P9-CBK-772

The Queen of Dreamland

INGRID TOMEY

ATHENEUM BOOKS FOR YOUNG READERS

Acknowledgments

To those who helped, to those who encouraged, I offer grateful thanks: to Scott Davidson who shared with me the trials and joys of life from a wheelchair; to all the warmhearted people I met through the Adoption Identity Movement of Michigan—the birth mothers, the adoptive parents, their sons and daughters, who so willingly told me their stories; to the wonderful women in Detroit Women Writers, who listened and encouraged. And, finally, to Ana Cerro, my editor, for her insight and unfailing wisdom.

Atheneum Books for Young Readers
An imprint of Simon & Schuster Children's Publishing Division
1230 Avenue of the Americas
New York, New York 10020

Book design by Becky Terhune
The text of this book is set in Perpetua.

First Edition
Printed in the United States of America
10 9 8 7 6 5 4 3 2 1

Library of Congress Cataloging-in-Publication Data
Tomey, Ingrid.
The Queen of Dreamland / by Ingrid Tomey.—1st ed.
p. cm.
Summary: After she discovers her birth mother, fourteen-year-old Julie
is torn between her feelings for the parents who adopted her and the Queen of Dreamland.
ISBN 0-689-80458-X
[1. Birth mothers—Fiction. 2. Adoption—Fiction.] I. Title.

PZ7.T5844Qu 1996
[Fic]—dc20 95-52363

For Ashley, whoever you are

I

It all started on Julie's fourteenth birthday—the year, the day, the hour that she was so tired of herself she tried to pretend she was someone else. Megan had suggested she try it. As if Megan could possibly know what it was like to see something so sorry-looking staring back at herself in the mirror, Julie thought. Still, she tried it.

Julie sat on the wide bathroom counter upstairs, her feet in the bathroom sink, the shower on hyper-jet behind her. For a moment, she just sat there, studying the pieces of her face like someone sizing up a difficult puzzle. Then she got to work. With a vibrant shade of red Julie colored in her thin, pale lips. She took off her glasses and clutched back her yellow hair. Then holding an invisible microphone under her chin with the other hand, she looked deep into her own eyes and broke into song.

"Oh, girl of my dreams, you are tender as dewww—your eyes are as bright as the sun—" For such a small person, Julie's voice was booming; she almost drowned out the shower. "Your hair is a shimmering bonnet of starrrrs—"

Despite the enthusiastic start, Julie stopped, her pale brows coming together in a sharp frown. Her eyes, she thought, were nothing like the sun. They were like dust—two gray balls of dust. Julie looked away, down at the dirt streaks her tennis shoes had left in the sink.

"Julie!" Her mother was rapping on the door. "I hope you aren't going to be much longer, dear. Your father is at the table, fork in hand."

Julie jerked around to make sure the door was locked. Mrs. Solus was famous for barging in uninvited. "Hang on," she yelled over the shower. "I'm just finishing up here."

"Well, hurry please. This is a special dinner, you know."

Julie sat curled up near the sink until she heard her mother's heavy footsteps going down the stairs. Finally, she picked up her feet and climbed down. "Baboon," she muttered, though her face resembled a baboon even less than her eyes looked like sunbeams. Julie was as disgusted with her gullibility as she was with her pale, bony face, her pointed nose, and her dust-colored eyes. She had believed Megan, her once best friend, when she said that singing to herself in the mirror could help Julie overcome what Megan called Julie's "negative concept."

Yanking at a piece of toilet paper to wipe her glasses with, she pulled the roll right off the spinner, spilling peach-colored toilet paper all over the floor. Julie kicked at it irritably, as if it were the source of all her misery. While other birthday girls were enjoying noisy sleepovers with their friends or eating out in fancy restaurants as guest of honor, Julie felt down. Singing in the mirror, she realized, was not going to transform her life.

When she opened the bathroom door, a blast of cool air hit Julie's face, as if she had just left some steamy jungle and returned suddenly to the real world. The grandfather clock was ticking in the foyer downstairs, ticking away the minutes of her dreary life. She could hear her mother pouring ice water into the good crystal goblets.

Poised at the top of the stairs, Julie hesitated, knowing her parents were waiting, yet dreading the celebration they had prepared. It seemed silly to her. The whole thing seemed silly to her—the candles, the singing, her mother's speech. It seemed like the fuss was for someone else. Someone she didn't even know. Taking a deep breath, Julie started down the stairs.

"Surprise!" the only two people in the room yelled when Julie entered the dining room. Mrs. Solus rushed forward to put the birthday crown on Julie's head and then stepped back, beaming. She was a large woman, big breasted, round in the stomach and everywhere else, with a florid face that got even redder when she was excited. Her eyes, a bright cinnamon color, surveyed her daughter lovingly. She had created the silver birthday crown years ago, patiently gluing on the stars and the little colored shells as if she was making the real thing. Mrs. Solus was a fusser, never quite satisfied with the amount of starch in her husband's shirts or with the way her floribunda roses dropped petals on a hot day. But she reserved her greatest fussing for Julie. From the instant Mrs. Solus became a mother, she devoted herself to making certain Julie was happy, safe, and well stuffed.

Julie's father was not so hovering as Mrs. Solus but he was no less devoted. When Julie was a toddler he used to piggyback her to town every Saturday morning to see the old-fashioned organ grinder and his monkey at the farmers' market. He would spend the morning sitting on dirty crates in his suit and tie, feeding Julie quarters to drop in the monkey's hat. At fourteen, Julie's tastes were more expensive, but he was just as committed to pleasing her. Now, he waved his fork at Julie, directing her to a chair at the end of the gleaming mahogany table that was tied with red balloons.

"The shower was on so long we were starting to build an ark down here. Let's eat," he said abruptly. He, too, was a large person, over six feet tall, but without the bulk of Julie's mother. He was a slow and patient man except when it came to his meals, which he insisted be served at seven-thirty A.M., noon, and six P.M. "Your mother has made—"

"Alpine potato soup, mini-meatballs, baby carrots, and candlestick salad," Julie recited. She gave her father a limp smile. "Same menu for fourteen years."

"Thirteen, dear." Mrs. Solus came in with three bananas stuck upright in rings of pineapple. "You were still eating baby food at a year." She set the candlestick salads around the table and popped a maraschino cherry on top of each one. "Remember, Wayne? Remember those days? Oh, Julie, I wish you could have seen yourself. You were as skinny as a farm kitten when we first got you. Remember, Wayne?" She sighed. "I really miss those baby days." She sat down and folded her hands.

"Well, now we've got teenager days," he said practically. Without pausing he went on, "For what we are about to receive may we be truly thankful, amen."

Her mother shook out her napkin and smiled at Julie. "Fourteen years old. I can't believe how the years sail by." She patted Julie's hand. "Did they sing 'Happy Birthday' to you at school?"

"'Happy Birthday'?" Julie asked, stabbing her banana with her fork. "In my classes?"

"Well, people can still remember your birthday even when you're as ancient as fourteen. When I was in school—"

"Never mind, Mother." Mr. Solus was less willing than his wife to glorify the past, notwithstanding his love of history. He looked at Julie, sensing that she wasn't exactly in a celebrating mood. "Where's your friend Megan? Doesn't she usually appear when there's a birthday cake to be disposed of?"

Mrs. Solus put her hand to her breast. "Megan," she gasped. "Oh, sweetheart, did Megan forget your birthday?"

The reminder of Megan gave Julie an extra spurt of annoyance. "Naturally, she didn't forget my birthday," she snapped, picking up her goblet so fast that water slopped on the tablecloth. "She doesn't exactly live and die for candlestick salad."

Mrs. Solus stopped beaming and turned to her food.

"Leave her alone, Mother," Mr. Solus said. "She just wanted to spend her birthday with dear old Mom and Dad."

"Dear old Mom and Dad," Julie mumbled. She felt the back of her neck get hot because that was irritating her, too. Her mother and father were both fifty-six years old, nearly twenty years older than the parents of most of her friends. And most of the time they acted even older. Both of them wore bedroom slippers from morning to night. Flop, flop, flop. She could hear them coming from any room in the house. Some days, when her father's bunions were acting up he even wore slippers when he was with patients. It made the hair on her arms stand up just thinking about it. So did the toilet paper her mother wrapped around her hair every night to keep it in shape. Julie tried to get her to change her hairstyle plenty of times, but her mother insisted on hair that looked like a roll of gray shredded wheat.

But when her mother set a stack of presents down by her plate, Julie was stricken with guilt. Her father was the most generous man on the face of the earth. Even if he did wear his bedroom slippers every day of his life he was better than all of her friends' fathers put together. And although her mother's hair looked like baling wire, it didn't keep her from baking snickerdoodles for Julie's lunch every week or from sitting up late helping her diagram sentences.

"This is great soup," she said to her mother. She took a big slurp of the hot potato broth and smiled. "Really great." She put her spoon down and opened her first present. It was from her father—a large, ornate brooch. Julie looked at the enormous ten-rayed star sprinkled with little garnets and opals and then back at her father. "What's this?"

"Your father picked that out from Celadon's because it was such an unusual piece." Her mother lifted Julie's soup bowl and mopped some spilled water from her plate. "It's by that Detroit artist with only one name—Navetti, Bagetti, something like that." She frowned. "That lipstick is a bit lurid, isn't it?"

"Thanks, Dad," Julie said. She put the top back on the box and sighed quietly. It was wrong, she thought. A terrible present that she would never wear. Too ugly for words. To Julie it looked like something one of the eighty-year-olds would wear out at Springhill Nursing Home, where she played the piano. Somehow, the brooch made her feel even worse than before—she felt like bursting into tears. But she forced herself to speak cheerfully. "I'm just not sure I'll have anyplace to wear it."

"Umm." Her father pinched his nostrils together. "I thought you said she'd like it, Mother." When it came to gifts, Mr. Solus was totally ruled by his wife. He had no objection to the price of anything as long as he knew it would please Julie.

"Oh, she will—you will, darling." Her mother leaned over and patted her cheek. "Maybe you're a little too young at fourteen but by the time you're twenty-one, you'll treasure such a beautiful jewel."

Now Mr. Solus brightened. "Think of it as an investment, Julie. A piece like this is a hedge against inflation. Even if you never wear it, you can visit it at the bank," he said, cheerful once more. Over the years, Mr. Solus's talent for maximizing his investments had managed to insure a comfortable lifestyle for his family. He leaned forward and stared at Julie. "Do this." He stretched his lips back over his teeth.

"Da-a-ad." But she knew there was no sense objecting. She grimaced, showing her teeth.

"Have you been flossing?"

Mr. Solus was a dentist. He examined everyone's teeth the same way. From this he could tell how well or how poorly people lived their lives. Unlike Julie, he didn't see this as an obsession but merely an outgrowth of his profession. Shoe salesmen looked at people's shoes, manicurists at people's hands. Mr. Solus was interested in teeth. He loved teeth. And Julie's teeth were a reflection on him. Automatically, Julie nodded and turned back to her gifts.

There was a fifty-dollar bill from Grandma Snoudy, which was really from Mr. and Mrs. Solus. They couldn't bear for Julie to think that her grandmother, who couldn't even recognize herself in the mirror anymore, couldn't remember her granddaughter. Next was a sweatshirt that Mrs. Solus had embroidered with a ring of pink-and-white daisies, Julie's name in green vines in the center. It was the sort of thing Mrs. Solus specialized in—floral embroidery—in much the same way she embroidered their yard with every kind of shrub and flower. The sweatshirt was, Julie thought, too cute. Mentally, she tucked it in a bottom drawer and left it there. She sighed again and unwrapped a crystal teddy bear, a wool blazer with matching slacks and skirt, and finally, a bottle of perfume. "Oh, 'Identity,' " she said, her spirits lifting. "This is the best, Mom."

"I got the biggest bottle they had."

Julie unscrewed the cap and sniffed. She wrinkled her nose. "Are you sure I said 'Identity'? Are you sure I didn't say 'Wistful'?"

"Well, I don't think so. No. I had the very same piece of paper in my purse to show to the clerk at Demerest's. 'Identity'—that's what you wrote down." She frowned. "Don't you like it?"

"Oh, it's great," Julie said, screwing the gold cap back on. "Maybe I'm getting a cold." When Julie had smelled the perfume on the model at Demerest's it had reminded her of the singer Etta Jonas at the Scarlett Supper Club. Julie had been there for dinner with her mom and dad and had watched Etta at the keyboard in her red, backless gown, her black hair clipped behind one ear with three diamonds. When Julie went up to the piano to give her a song request, Etta smelled just how she looked—sultry and mysterious. Just like the model in Demerest's smelled. Only now, sitting at the table with her parents, the perfume didn't smell sultry and mysterious. Julie sniffed again. It smelled like bubble gum, she thought.

Her mother dimmed the chandelier and brought in a big cake from Winfrey's Bakery, glowing with candles. Her parents sang "Happy Birthday", her mother's voice high and quivery, her father's husky and off-key. Julie groaned. She knew what was coming.

Mrs. Solus stood up, brushing crumbs off her large bosom. Then she and Julie's father lifted their water goblets like they were toasting the Queen of England. "Now, Julie, don't look so tortured," her mother said, beaming down at her. "You know your birthday is very special to your father and me." Her expression became more sober as she began the speech she made, with minor variations, every year.

"Saturday was your calendar birthday, the day fourteen years ago that you came into the world. And that is a miracle day for us because you were born—a perfect, beautiful, little blond-haired baby with perfect fingers and toes, big gray eyes, everything, just everything about you so perfect. But this day, today—" Mrs. Solus's eyes were suddenly brimming.

"Today," she repeated, "is the anniversary of the real miracle to your father and me. This is the day we adopted that perfect, little blond baby, that beautiful soul, our daughter who has brightened our lives and lifted our hearts for fourteen years. We could give you a hundred gifts, sweetheart, a million gifts, and it wouldn't compare to the gifts you have given us over the years. Gifts of joy, of . . ."

Julie jiggled her knees under the table and silently counted backward from one hundred.

"—and most of all," Mrs. Solus continued, dabbing at her eyes, "most of all, the gift of love. Happy birthday, darling."

Julie took off the aluminum crown, leaned toward the cake, and in one hot breath whooshed out all the candles.

"Did you make a wish?" her mother asked.

Julie shoved over Jacquelina, her mannequin, and curled up in the window seat, thinking about what she wished. She wished Megan hadn't fallen madly in love with bull-necked Charlie Robeson. She wished she had pink cheeks instead of looking like the bride of Dracula, that she was known as "The Songbird of Oakland County," and that she had bosoms. She wished that her father didn't wear bedroom slippers at work and that her mother didn't try to crawl inside her head. Most of all, she wished she knew who Juliana Blanche Solus was.

She knew she wasn't the fairy tale princess her mom and dad toasted every birthday. She was ungrateful and crabby and bored stiff eating mini-meatballs and playing "Meet Me in St. Louie, Louie," every night for her father after dinner. And she wasn't like Megan, either—gorgeous and giggly and smelling like Hudson's Aisles of Beauty, with a little sister at home who was just as giggly and gorgeous as she was.

She had nobody—no brothers or sisters, no cousins, and only an ancient grandmother who could barely talk anymore. And she felt like a total alien with her mom and dad. They reminded her of old horses plodding around and around in the same circle day after day. They had to have everything just a certain way—the drapes closed promptly at six P.M., pork roast and potatoes on Monday nights, veal picata on Tuesdays, channel seven news from six to seven, red roses in the foyer. Julie wanted to scream. She wanted to dump the perfect roses all over the perfect salmon-and-green Chinese rug. She wanted to fly into a million pieces and turn into real silver stars and fall out of the sky, breaking people's windows all over the universe.

Julie stared out the window at the whirling snow. She should have been born in July, she thought, when all the flowers were in bloom, instead of in January, the loneliest month in the year. If she had been a July baby she might have been beautiful, she might be playing the piano for thousands of dollars at the Scarlett Supper Club instead of volunteering at Springhill Nursing Home. She would have thousands of friends and they would send each other witty cards and tasteful, expensive presents.

She looked underneath her dresser, where she had shoved the clutter of stuffed animals her father had given her over the years. Now he had gone to the other extreme. She picked up the big gaudy pin and wondered what had made her father think she would ever wear such a thing. She stared down at it. Would she? Did her mother and father see someone who would one day wear this ugly, clunky pin and think it was beautiful? How could she feel one way one year and another way the next?

Julie stuck the pin into a tangle of Jacquelina's orange hair, then tied her blue bandanna over it. For a moment she sat there holding the old mannequin against her chest. Four years ago, Julie had pulled Jacquelina from the trash bin behind Crowley's Dress Boutique and brought her home, dressing her in an old party dress Julie didn't wear anymore. Julie used to whisper secrets to Jacquelina at night, pretending she was a little sister. Now, even though she was too old for pretend games, Julie still talked to her, especially when she was upset. "Who am I?" she murmured to Jacquelina. She looked at her murky reflection in the darkening window. Julie let go of Jacquelina and flung herself across the bed. "Who am I?"

For the dozenth time Julie took out the little yellow card she had hidden beneath her pillow. Someone had stuffed it into the vent hole of her locker at school. COME TO DREAMLAND. FIND OUT WHO YOU ARE AND WHERE YOU ARE GOING. PALMS READ, DREAMS INTERPRETED. A rainbow arched across the front of the card, with a pot of gold at one end. And on the back, in a barely readable scrawl, was a message: *Dear Julie, For your 14th birthday come to Dreamland and have your palm read for free! Find out all the secrets of your life! xoxoxoxoxoxoxo Loretta Young.*

2

The trip from Canopy to Potatoville was only eleven miles but for Julie it was like traveling to the other side of the moon. Through the window of the bus she watched the snow-covered street unwind like a spool of white thread. Just inches past her face, snow whirled in confused eddies, like her heart whirling and leaping in her chest.

She looked away, at the man sitting next to her. His head hung forward so that his chin touched his chest. His red face was covered with spiky black hairs as if he hadn't shaved in days. Worse than the way he looked was the way he smelled—like someone had broken a bottle of beer over his head. At nine o'clock in the morning, Julie was sitting next to a drunk man on a bus going to Potatoville. Her mother would be tracking the bus in a police car if she knew.

As her mother handed her the twenty dollars for her piano lesson she went through the spiel that began every Saturday morning before Julie went off on the bus and Mrs. Solus set out for Griffinville. "Do you have quarters for the bus?"

Julie nodded.

"Do you have your books?"

Julie pulled her piano books out of her green Harrod's bag and held up "Edith McIntosh's A Dozen a Day," "Burgmuller," and "Show Tunes of the '60s."

Mrs. Solus kissed the top of Julie's head. "You've got fifteen minutes to catch the nine o'clock bus. Now make sure your lesson is over precisely at ten-thirty so you'll have plenty of time to get the eleven o'clock bus. You know how Mrs. Wigmore is. She can get started talking about her Siamese cats and you'll never get away. She caught me once in the grocery store—" Mrs. Solus glanced at her watch. "Whoops—I've got to get going, too. Dad expects you there by noon. That will give you time to stop at Wong Lee's for the egg rolls. Now don't forget to call me up north. I should be at Grandma's nursing home by twelve. If for some reason I'm not—"

"I know, I know," Julie said. "They'll give you the message." They went through this routine every week, ever since Mrs. Solus started making the three-hour trip north every weekend to visit her ailing mother. Julie was sentenced to spend every Saturday afternoon at her father's office, eating Chinese carryout, licking stamps on envelopes, and counting out rubber gloves and floss and toothbrushes. Her mother's last words before they both went out the door were always the same. "And, Julie, be careful."

Now her mother's repeated warnings rang in her ears. Being careful, she knew, meant not sitting next to bums, bag ladies, the kinds of people who sat alone on park benches and drank from bottles in paper bags. But the man had gotten on after she had and slumped down beside her. She glanced sideways, wondering if she should slide past him and find another seat. He was so greasy and ratty, she thought. She could see his elbow sticking through a hole in his jacket.

Clutching her piano books to her chest, she fixed her eyes on a bus ad for air conditioners. "My heart is like a comet—" Julie started singing softly and snapping the rubber band she wore on her wrist. When she was little Julie would twist and pull the sleeves of her sweaters so hopelessly out of shape when she was nervous that her mother put a rubber band on her wrist to break her of the habit. She still put the rubber band on every morning the way other people put on their watches because her life was full of nerve-racking moments. This was one of them.

Julie took the little yellow card out of her pocket and looked at it again, cupping it in her hand so the man couldn't read it, in case he was watching her out of his slitted eyes. "Dreamland," she whispered. "Palms read, dreams interpreted. Find out who you are and where you are going." She turned it over and passed her fingers back and forth over the words on the back. "Find out all the secrets of your life!"

She took a deep breath. Her heart hammered in her chest as if it was squeezed into a tiny box. What kinds of secrets? she wondered, nervously plinking her rubber band. Something, she was certain, something was about to happen. It was the feeling she used to get at the Oakland County Fair, scared witless and excited to tears at the same time. She closed her eyes and the bus turned into a carnival ride. Riding straight up, in the nose of the Bullet, red lights whirling on either side of her, she could dive-bomb back to earth or shoot upward into endless space like a fiery comet. Her eyes still closed, she started singing another Springhill song, "It's a day to make hay, get out of the way—"

Julie jumped when the man next to her snorted. She leaned away from him, pressing herself against the window. Without meaning to she conjured up a vision of Mrs. Wigmore's sweating, red face, snapping out the rhythm of "Rage over a Lost Penny" with her fingers. What if Mrs. Wigmore discovers she had lied about having a sprained finger? she thought. There was that time two years ago when Julie tipped over a vase of flowers onto the piano keys and Mrs. Wigmore sent her home. Would she throw Julie out once and for all? What if she asks to look at Julie's finger? Julie took off her mittens and studied her ten perfectly good fingers. Mrs. Wigmore would insist on checking next Saturday and she would see that there was absolutely no stiffness, no swelling. Why hadn't Julie said she had a visiting relative or a new kitten or that she had dropped her glasses in the compactor?

"Penny Lane," the driver called. Julie caught her breath. She stood up, spilling her piano books into the aisle. When she bent over she stepped on Beer Breath's foot. He looked down at her out of his thin yellow eyes, like a wolf.

"This is Penny Lane," she repeated stupidly, as if that explained her clumsiness. She grabbed her books and dashed out the rear exit.

She stood on the corner looking down Penny Lane, the snow stinging her face and blowing into the back of her coat. She yanked up her collar and felt in her pockets for her mittens. "Oh, fudruckers," she said, which was the name of the grill where her father had lunch. She watched now as the red-and-white bus carrying her mittens disappeared into the twirling snow.

Julie turned and looked the other way down Penny Lane, trying to decide on a direction. She was standing near a saggy little restaurant with a swinging sign next to the door that said, HOME OF THE POTATO BURGER. In the restaurant parking lot someone was working under the hood of a big old yellow-and-black junker—she could just see his legs. The sound of metal banging against metal rang out in the stillness as she looked beyond the car to a sprinkling of little box houses. They all looked mean and cold in the storm. Down the other way Julie could see nothing except for a big, white house, almost lost against the gray sky, and beyond that, acres and acres of empty potato fields.

"Aay—whatcha looking for?"

Julie turned to see the person that belonged to the legs. He had black curly hair tied around with a dirty white bandanna and he was tossing a wrench from one hand to the other.

"What's the address?" he said, crossing one long leg over the other and holding out his hand, as if he knew about the yellow card in her pocket.

"I'm going that way," Julie said and she started running before he had a chance to say another word. She looked over her shoulder but he just stood there leaning against the car, grinning. She stopped running and plodded through the snow toward the big, white house, wondering what she would do if it wasn't the right address. If she had to turn around he had better stay under the hood and mind his own business.

It was an enormous house, three stories high, with chimneys at both ends and a long sweep of stairs leading up to a porch that extended its entire width. At one end of the porch under fresh mounds of snow were a small, round luncheon table and four chairs, huddled together like forgotten children. At this point, the house rounded out, all three stories, ending at the top in a cone-shaped room overgrown with vines. Julie looked up at this little room and thought of *Sparkina the Alien,* a movie she had seen five times. When Sparkina fell to earth she had been imprisoned for three years in the round tower of an old house. As Julie stood there trying to see if there were bars on the windows, a huge black dog came bounding around the corner of the house and lunged at her, knocking her face first into the snow.

Julie spit snow out of her mouth and screamed before the dog pounced on her again. She screamed again. "Help! Oh God, oh please. Help me!" She held out her arms to fend him off.

"Winston! You naughty boy, get in here, Winston. I'm going to give you a licking, Winston, if you don't get off her right this minute. Sorry, hon," the woman yelled from the doorway. "He thinks you want to play."

"Get him away from me!" Julie hollered. "He's trying to kill me!"

In a second the woman was outside and had Winston by the ear. "Why can't you behave?" she hissed at the dog. She slapped him on the rear and he went galloping through the snow and in the front door. "Come on in," she said to Julie, taking her hand and pulling her up.

Julie jammed her snow-covered glasses back in place and glared at the woman. But she kept hold of Julie's hand and shook it vigorously. "I'm Loretta Young. Glad to meet ya."

The woman who had taken hold of Julie's hand was maybe thirty and didn't look like anyone's idea of a palm reader. Instead of looking like a ruffly skirted gypsy, Loretta Young was dressed like someone on her way to a New Year's Eve party. Her tight, gold jumpsuit was decorated, front and back, with rows of cherry-colored buttons and her small stature was augmented by three-inch heels on black suede boots. There was something even more exotic-looking about her gray eyes—they were fringed with vibrant purple lashes, in the same shade of purple as her fingernails. Julie noticed the false eyelashes when Loretta squatted down to brush snow off Julie's pant legs. Julie stepped back. In her fourteen years she had never seen anyone with purple eyelashes. "I've got to catch the bus," she said.

"Might's well have the reading then," Loretta Young said, tugging her toward the house. "Won't be a bus for another hour."

She had come this far. And it was too cold to stand out on the corner for the next hour, so Julie followed her. When she got to the threshold, though, she froze. "Where's that dog?"

"Oh, Winston's gone to the pantry. He always goes there to snooze after his romp. He's really very nice, Winston is. Wouldn't hurt a midge."

"I hate dogs. They smell bad and they're vicious." As soon as she said it, Julie realized she sounded just like her mother.

Loretta Young seemed undisturbed by Julie's aversion to her dog. "Put it right out of your mind," she said, waving her purple nails through the air and leading Julie across a huge, messy room that smelled like saltwater taffy.

Julie unwound her scarf and wiped the snow off her glasses, glancing up at the high ceiling. The flowered wallpaper had started peeling, revealing a different floral pattern underneath. Sheets of colored paper were scattered about like autumn leaves, as well as pieces of string and empty coffee cups. There were some old pieces of furniture—too ruined to be called antiques—a tall cabinet with a cracked, frosted door on which a dancing lady was etched and next to that an ornate, Chippendale chair with a stained red velvet seat. Two orange beanbag chairs sat opposite a long, rickety-looking table holding some notebooks and three black telephones. Behind the table was a huge painted sign of a giant rainbow and the words THE QUEEN OF DREAMLAND.

"This way," Loretta Young said, pushing aside the tail of a kite that was hanging from the ceiling. "Right this way."

Julie looked around uneasily as she followed Loretta Young through an orange-painted door. When she glanced back she saw two old people standing in a doorway at the opposite end of the living room. They were just standing there, not saying a word, watching her like they had been expecting her. The feeling it gave her was unnerving, like she was a little bug under a microscope. She suddenly wanted to bolt and run. But Loretta Young took her by the arm and nudged her into a folding chair. Settling herself in the other one, she leaned back, running her fingers through her curly, blond hair. "Good timing," she said. "I always get a resurgence about midmorning. My phenomes are at their peak."

Julie felt for her rubber band. In this room there were no walls, no windows, only shimmering orange fabric draped from floor to ceiling. She felt a million miles from home, in the tent of some Arabian sheik. She forgot the feeling of the carnival ride, the feeling of wanting to burst into space like a blazing comet. Looking at Loretta Young's purple eyelashes, she suddenly didn't care a bit what her future held. She never should have come, never should have lied to Mrs. Wigmore. This whole thing was a big mistake.

Loretta Young reached over and grabbed her hand.

"Uhh!" Julie jumped.

"Just relax, hon." Loretta Young patted her knee.

Julie pulled her hand away and jumped to her feet. "I've changed my mind. I don't want my fortune told, I don't want my palm read. Just let me out of here!"

Loretta Young closed her eyes so that her long purple lashes rested against her cheeks. "Oh, hon," she said. Then she looked up at Julie for a long, sorrowful moment. "Jewel."

Julie had her hand on the doorknob but she paused. "Julie," she said hotly. "My name is Julie."

Loretta Young shook her head. "Your name is Jewel."

3

Julie stood there for a long, breathless moment, staring at the woman with the purple eyelashes. "What?" she said, clutching the doorknob.

"I should know," Loretta Young said. "I gave it to you."

Julie's hand went limp as she turned back into the room. "Gave—me—"

"Your name—Jewel. They changed it to Julie, I guess. Who can blame them? It's like anything new. You wanna name it yourself."

Julie stared at Loretta Young, trying to understand what she was saying. But the more she stared, the more she couldn't see her. Her blond hair, her purple eyelashes, the gold jumpsuit, the orange walls—all started to merge into a whirlpool of color. The room was like a great, spinning galaxy sucking Julie into its center. She felt herself whirling so fast her ears were ringing. And then, as if she had suddenly been released, she stopped and wobbled slowly to the floor.

"Mrs. Og! Cramp! Mrs. Og!" She heard Loretta Young's voice yelling from far away and then another voice, lightly accented but sweet as honey, right next to her ear. "Candy Lamb, vake up, Candy Lamb. You just had a tiny startle, Sugar Pie. Now open your eyes."

When Julie did she saw three faces hovering over her. One was Loretta Young, who looked like a bright flower that had suddenly folded in on itself. Her face was pale and she clutched at her hair in silence. The other two faces belonged to the old man and the old lady who had been watching from the doorway.

"Dere she comes, Loretta," said the old lady. "I know it. You were too sudden vit her. I know it. Don't I tell you"—she shook a fat finger— "break it to her gentle, nice and gentle. But no—you goose. Go get her some seltzer," she said to the old man. He rose obediently from the floor and disappeared.

Julie sat up and blinked, shaking her head to clear it. "I didn't really faint," she said. "I think I sort of fell down." She looked at Loretta Young and her voice evaporated. "Are you," she whispered, "are you—"

Loretta Young clutched at her hair and nodded, her fringed eyes as wide as daisies. "I'm your mother."

Julie turned to the other woman who was as plump and squishy-looking as a stuffed doll. A mass of snow white hair was piled like whipped cream on top of her head. In fact, everything she had on was white, right down to her shoes. "Are you a nurse?" Julie asked.

"No, Honeycakes," she said, in her soft foreign accent. She took Julie's face between her hands and smiled an enormous smile. "I am Mrs. Og, a baker and telephone answer lady." Before Julie could take this in, the old man came back with the seltzer water, which Mrs. Og handed to Julie.

"Dis is Cramp," Mrs. Og said, pulling in the reluctant old man with her arm. "Handyman, trainer, gardener. He helps vit Bagley Vonder."

Cramp was tall. His head nearly touched the folds of drapery that hung from the center of the ceiling. He wore his gray hair pulled back in a wiry ponytail. That and the diamond in his right ear gave him the look of an old rebel. Julie noticed the earring and she also noticed his left ear, what there was of it. It had met with some injury, as had the entire left side of his face, which was as dented as the surface of the moon.

He bowed at Julie and left the room without saying a word.

"I fix us sometink nice to eat. Some very good potato pancakes, eh?" Mrs. Og smiled eagerly at Julie. "Vat you say, eh?"

Julie finished the water and handed the glass back. She shook her head. "I have to go back. My mother is expecting me to—" A sudden brightness flashed in her head like a burst of fireworks. She was *with* her mother. She looked at Loretta Young.

As if she had read Julie's mind, Loretta Young stopped tugging on her hair and her lips turned up in a quick smile.

"Vell, girls—I got a raspberry torte in da oven so I leave you now." Mrs. Og flapped her white apron at Julie and went out the door.

Mrs. Og left them still sitting on the floor. Julie looked at Loretta Young in her shimmering gold jumpsuit, her blond hair bushing out all around her head like an exploded dandelion. Then she noticed the perfume. It smelled like saltwater taffy. Julie started to feel woozy again, like she had just come out of the hall of mirrors. She put her hand out and felt the smooth orange fabric draped all around her. She pinched it between her fingers. Was it real? Was any of it real? she wondered.

"Hey—" Loretta Young reached out and poked her arm. "Happy birthday."

She looked back at Loretta. "You—did you put that in my locker? That card?"

"Sure—hey, I'm going to have a stick of gum. My mouth gets like a desert when I'm nervous, you know?" She pulled a pack of Juicy Fruit from her breast pocket and held it out. "Want some?"

Julie shook her head, surprised to hear Loretta Young was nervous. "How do you know me? That I'm—that you're—"

"Well, first of all" —Loretta Young unpeeled the gum and curled it up like a bedroll before popping it in her mouth— "you have a boomerang on your left elbow—just above it. Leastwise you did when you were born." She held her finger and thumb up, an inch apart. "A little brown boomerang. Still got it?"

Julie clutched the place above her elbow where the birthmark was. Then, turning away from Loretta Young, she pulled up the sleeve of her sweater and twisted her arm to look at it.

"There!" Loretta Young crawled around on her knees and pointed. "Just like a little old boomerang," she said, with a deep Southern country twang.

"Crescent moon," Julie murmured, examining the faded brown mark. "That's what my mom calls it."

Loretta sat back on her heels. "And, second of all, you're the spitting image of me."

Julie's mouth dropped open. She couldn't imagine that there was any comparison between her wispy, faded looks and Loretta Young with her bright cheeks, bouncy hair, and glamorous figure.

"We got the same hair—" She reached out and rubbed the ends of Julie's hair. "You could use a good perm. We got the exact same eyes—April mist gray, I call them and look, even the same eyelashes." She burst into giggles at Julie's expression. "I don't mean these—I mean the ones underneath. Stubby as pig bristles, aren't they? Ya oughta try some purple ones."

Julie looked at her cautiously. She thought false eyelashes were for movie stars and nightclub singers.

"Or orange," Loretta Young said, giggling and punching Julie's arm.

Loretta Young was joking. When Julie realized it, the tight-fisted feeling in her stomach dissolved and she was able to manage a little smile.

"Forlorn as little pig bristles," Loretta Young said again, pointing at Julie's eyelashes. Julie snorted. Then she started to laugh; before she knew it she was laughing so hard she was almost crying. She felt her insides crumple up like wet toilet paper. She wrapped her arms around herself and doubled over, feeling excited and scared and happy and sad all at once. Finally, wiping her cheeks with the back of her hand, she asked the question that had leaped up into her throat. "Why did you—"

"Why did I contact you?" Loretta stretched gum over her teeth and sucked in, making little popping noises. "Well, you know I'm an interpreter of dreams. People call me up and go, 'I've been having this dream about falling down an elevator shaft,' or 'My hair is gone totally gray,' so I tell them, 'Look at your life. What's on your mind? Are you afraid of something?' Especially if they keep having the same dream. So" —Loretta delicately licked the tips of her index fingers and continued— "I started having this dream over and over. It was about finding a diamond—a perfect, glittering diamond. I must have had that dream fifty or two hundred times. I'd be walking along the sidewalk just minding my own business and bing—that big old diamond would pop up right in front of me. It was a message—I was going to find you. You know, my lost jewel. And" —-she looked at Julie and held out her arms— "here you are."

Julie shook her head. "No, I mean, geeze—" She looked down at the floor, mortified. For fourteen years the question had perched like a hungry crow at the back of her mind. She took a deep breath. "Why did you give me away?"

Loretta Young gasped and her face flooded with color. "Oh, crud on a crutch, I didn't want to, Jewel. Oh, it pritneer broke my heart into smithereens to give you up." She put her hands to her cheeks. "Have you been wondering about that all your life? Oooh, it's made you miserable, hasn't it?"

Julie blinked. A neon sign lit up in her head. It had been there forever but she tried not to look at it, or think about it. It was too awful. ABANDONED, the sign said. She had been abandoned, cast away, like a pebble on the beach, like a piece of litter, like any old rotten apple. ABANDONED, ABANDONED, ABANDONED, the sign had blinked throughout her entire life. Through the nights when she awoke, scared from a dream, through the days when everyone else was chosen for soccer while she stood alone against the gym wall, left over, unwanted. And here she was with the only person who knew. Who understood. Julie nodded.

"Aw, Jewel." Loretta wrung her hands. "It wasn't that I didn't love you. Because I really, truly did. But I was a seventeen-year-old kid—not even out of high school, see, and I didn't have a job and my old man kicked me right out of the house when I got PG so I didn't even have a place to stay, never mind take care of a baby, so I said, what's the best thing I can do for my precious little Jewel? And the best thing was to turn you over to a fine, rich man and lady who would give you absolutely everything. Don't you see?" She sat down on the floor again and earnestly clasped Julie's hand between her own. "See what I'm saying, Jewel?"

Julie stared at Loretta Young's slender hands wound around hers and remembered all the times she tried to imagine a younger, livelier mother, someone who would go out shopping in shorts or who would hit tennis balls with her the way Megan's mother did. Because Julie's mother had told her that much—that her birth mother was very young. She always said it sadly, as though it were a fatal disease. "Your mother was very, very young, dear."

"I always tried to picture you," Julie said, doodling on the floor with her finger.

"Did you hate me? Oh, Jewel, please oh please say you didn't hate me. Did you?" Loretta Young squeezed her hand tighter.

Julie pushed her glasses up with her finger and thought about it.

"I wanted to know who you were. What you looked like." She looked into Loretta Young's gray eyes. "And I wondered if—did you ever think about me?"

"Oh, cheez—" Loretta got to her knees. "Every year on January eighteen, I sent you a birthday card."

"You sent me cards?" Julie asked. "I never got any cards."

Loretta shook her head, her blond curls flying. "It was mental. I would close my eyes and picture you at five years old, or ten, or whatever—a little girl with blond hair and gray eyes and I would imagine you surrounded by beautiful presents and a fancy smancy house with a swimming pool and a grand piano and tons of clothes and everything your heart could desire."

Julie's eyes opened wide. "I have all that," she said. "Everything you named."

"See." Loretta Young pointed a purple fingernail at her. "You did get my cards then."

Julie nodded slowly. It reminded her of something that happened when she was in the fourth grade. They were making Mother's Day cards and the teacher had asked the class to bring in photos of their mothers. Julie had cut out a picture from a magazine of a beautiful, golden-haired woman in a glittering red dress. She carried the card with the picture in her little plastic purse for a whole year to give to her real mother in case she ever ran into her on the street. Suddenly, she realized something. She *could* have run into her mother on the streets of Canopy and not even known it. "Have you always lived here?" Julie asked. "I mean, since I was born?"

"Naw," Loretta said. "I got married and then my husband, Sidney Wonder, died and me and Bagley moved here a couple years ago."

"Bagley Wonder?" Julie remembered that Mrs. Og had mentioned him.

“Oh, Jewel, you gotta meet Bagley. I almost forgot. And he’s been downstairs all this time. You just gotta meet my baby. Cramp will bring him up any minute.” She jumped up, her heels clicking against the wood floor.

Julie got up, too. “I have to go. Honest I do.” She looked at her watch. If she didn’t make it to her father’s office by noon her mother would probably call out the state police. “My mother worries.”

Loretta Young turned back to Julie, alert as a cat. “Where does she think you are?”

Julie picked up her piano books from the table and showed Loretta. “At my piano lesson.”

Loretta Young yanked at her hair. “Do you think she might get cheesed off about me getting in touch with you?”

Julie shrugged. She couldn’t tell Loretta Young the truth—that her mother would have apoplexy if she discovered where Julie had gone today.

“Be sure and come back,” Loretta said at the door. “Come back next Saturday and meet Bagley. We’ll celebrate,” she added, wiggling her fingers in the air.

Julie didn’t say yes and she didn’t say no. But she knew.

4

Julie hit the top of the alarm clock and fell back against her pillow. She opened her eyes and looked at the blue-and-white-checked wallpaper border running along the top of the bedroom walls, the vase of yellow flowers, the crystal zoo on top of her dresser. As her eyes traced the familiar patterns, she realized a sudden, breathtaking truth. Nothing in this room had one thing to do with her. Her entire life had changed. She didn't even feel the same anymore.

Lifting her arms from under the covers, she looked at them as if she had never seen them before. They weren't skinny, broomstick arms as she had always imagined. They were willowy arms, arms that could drip with diamonds, that could blow kisses over the railing of a ship. She sat up and twisted her left arm, studying the brown mark above her elbow. Realizing her real mother had looked at that very spot fourteen years ago, and had touched it, made her stop breathing for an instant. She touched it now and was filled with a vision of Loretta Young's hair, glowing like the sun.

Julie picked up her glasses from the nightstand, put them on, and swung her feet over the side of the bed. She sat there, bouncing up and down, staring at her toes, wondering what Loretta Young had thought of her. Julie examined herself in the full-length mirror opposite her bed, tilting her head to the left, to the right. Narrow, sharp-nosed, bony. It wasn't a face anyone would fight a duel over, not beautiful as her mother insisted it was. But it wasn't boring either. Maybe it could be called intriguing. But Loretta Young—*her mother*, thought Julie, thrilling at the sound of that phrase—Loretta Young *was* beautiful in a bold and colorful way. Hadn't she said Julie looked just like her? She threw back her head and smiled hugely, a Loretta Young smile.

"Julie—" Her mother knocked, then opened the door. "Are you up?"

Julie leaped up so fast she crashed into her dresser and fell back on the bed. "Yes," she said, jumping up again and yanking her underwear drawer open. "I'll be down in a jiffy."

"I'm going to start your father's breakfast. Do you want turkey bacon?"

Julie turned around. "Look at this little thing." She twisted her arm to show her mother. "Is it a birthmark?"

Her mother nodded. "Uh-hmm. You've had that since the day we brought you home. I always thought it looked like a tiny crescent moon, especially when you were little." She reached out and rubbed it lightly. "It's almost faded away."

"Well, do you think it looks like a boomerang?"

Her mother picked up a sweater from the floor and folded it over the back of a chair. "Julie, I've got to get the bacon started. Your father's downstairs already. Do you want some or not?"

Julie shook her head and her mother went to the door.

"Wait—"

Her mother turned, exasperated.

Julie looked at her mother—an overweight woman in a plaid

bathrobe with stiff, gray hair. She was like one of those older women in denture cream commercials, Julie thought, seeing with her new eyes. For the first time in her life she wasn't annoyed by her mother's appearance. She felt sorry for her. She had no style, no pizzazz at all. Her mother just looked worn out. "Mom?" Julie leaned forward and caught her hand.

Mrs. Solus pointed at the bell jar clock on Julie's dresser. "I have forty-five minutes to get you and your father off to your respective places. That means making sure you're awake, taking breakfast orders, cooking breakfast, pressing a shirt, a blouse, a pair of pants and, finally, getting you out the door. I'm sorry, but this is not the best time for chitchat."

"Oh. Well—" Julie let go of her mother's hand. "I was wondering if you could go easy on the mayo in my egg salad sandwich? It gooshes all over the place."

Julie sank back on the bed after her mother left. She tried to imagine telling her mother what had happened. Peeling off her pajamas, Julie tested several versions of Saturday's events. "Mother, I went to visit my mother today—my real mother." No, she thought, too heartless. "Mom, I went to see my other mother today." She considered it. No—too abrupt. She had to ease into it. "Mom, I went to see a lady on Saturday. Guess who?" She shook her head. It would never work. Though her parents never came right out and told her to shut up, they discouraged Julie from even mentioning her birth mother.

Maybe, she thought, standing in the shower, she could tell her mother that Loretta was a poor, uneducated, single mother who made her living telling fortunes in a tumble-down house in Potatoville. "No!" She flung her washcloth at the ceiling, where it caught on the light fixture and began dripping water down the mirror. She would not belittle Loretta Young to make her mother feel superior. She wouldn't do it for any reason. Loretta was beautiful and she was smart and interesting. Loretta was more interesting than her mother, Julie thought. While Loretta was reading people's palms, her mother was shuffling around in slippers, arranging roses in vases or out in the yard, digging up bulbs. Julie was sure her mother wouldn't like Loretta Young. She only liked people who were ordinary, who lived in houses where the furniture matched and the wallpaper stayed on the walls and who dressed like the dummies in the windows of The Village Shop.

It came to her like a slow fist pressing down on her heart. Her mother would try to keep her from seeing Loretta Young. "She has no right!" Julie hissed as she stepped out of the shower. In spite of her mother, she made up her mind. And, thinking of going to see Loretta again, Julie's stomach jumped all the way to her throat.

She went downstairs to practice her piano until breakfast was ready. She pushed back the fall board and ran a finger down the cool keys. It was like touching an old friend. She exhaled loudly. Ordinarily, she would play something light and lively. Harry Connick or one of the old people's songs—something she could sing along with to help get her mood jelled for the day. But this morning she started pounding as hard as she could, playing so loud that her mother came to the doorway.

"Play something else, dear. Your father is trying to read the paper."

"No—I can't stop! I have to practice this!" Julie yelled. "For my lesson." It wasn't a lie. In her present state, Julie couldn't stop. If she stopped she might make a running start for the plate-glass window and fling herself through it, out into the bitter cold, and then run and run and run in her stocking feet until her feet froze into two little blocks of ice and she couldn't run anymore. But even then, she knew, her heart would keep going—zooming around at a hundred miles per hour until she fell over dead.

"I'm from Borneo-eeo-eeo, I drink rat's blood—eeo-eeo, and crunch their bones—eeo—eeo, I sleep on thorns in Borneo. Eeeeoooo, eeeeoooo," Julie sang at the top of her lungs. It was her song—she had made it up to sing to the old people when they started nodding off in the Springhill rec room.

Her mother sighed. "Well, your father's not crazy about that piece, especially at seven in the morning. Do you want turkey bacon, Julie?"

"Crud on a crutch!" Julie slammed the keys with all ten fingers and turned on the bench. "I said no turkey bacon. I hate turkey bacon. How many times do I have to tell you?"

Instantly, her father's red face, his napkin tucked under his chin, appeared in the doorway. "You will either apologize to your mother or you will walk to school."

"Sorry," Julie muttered. But she wasn't sorry at all.

After her father dropped her at school Julie went to the cafeteria to think. She chose the table under the blower because is was so cold nobody ever sat there. Most of the kids were piled up around the donut counter. She looked at them, eating and talking and jumping around like seven-year-olds on Christmas morning. They had nothing better to think about than what kind of jelly they wanted in their donuts, she thought.

Julie put her hands on the table and looked at them. These hands belong to Jewel Young, she thought. She made a huge J with her finger on the green Formica tabletop. One big letter at a time, she wrote JEWEL YOUNG. "Jewel Young," she said out loud. "My name is Jewel Young."

She saw a boy from her history class staring at her from over by the juice bar. I'm not who you think I am, she thought, staring back at him. She wrote JEWEL YOUNG again across the table and looked back at the boy. But he was licking powdered sugar off his fingers and watching some other guy throw his lunch bag in the air.

Julie felt like a shimmery bubble floating high above the earth. The boy who had stared at her sat right in front of her in Mr. Annelin's class; now she couldn't even remember his name. All she could remember was her name. JEWEL YOUNG. Her life would never be the same. But, she thought, if she went to Clifford Smart Middle School every day and practiced the piano like always and flossed her teeth twice a day like always, how could anyone tell? How should she begin her new life? Julie looked at her hands again, palms up, palms down. They were different. Every cell of her was different.

"Julie, what are you doing back here?"

She looked up to see Megan, her perfect brown hair as shiny as silk under the fluorescent lights. She didn't want to seem too happy to see her; she was still mad that Megan had forgotten her birthday. In the seven years they had known each other they had never once missed each other's birthday. Until a month ago, she had consulted Megan on the smallest details of her life. Now, Charlie stood between them like a brick wall.

Julie scanned the room and looked back at Megan, who had sat down with her hot chocolate. "Where's Mr. Heartthrob?" Julie asked.

"He's got the flu—he's been barfing all weekend. I hope I don't get it. Yuk."

Even when Megan made a face, she looked beautiful. Her big, brown eyes got bigger, her mouth opened to reveal perfect, pearly teeth.

"Want some hot chocolate?"

Julie shook her head. "It's probably full of Charlie's cooties."

"I didn't even see him this weekend. I had to baby-sit for my parents on Saturday, and Sunday he was sick. I'm a widow." Megan sighed loudly, took out a comb from her purse, and began combing her hair. "Hey—did you try singing to yourself in the mirror?" she asked, instantly cheerful again.

"God, Megan." Julie shook her head. "What a dorky idea." She looked at Megan, wanting to stay mad at her but, even more, wanting to tell her everything. "Listen, you want to hear something funny?"

Megan nodded.

"My mother—" Julie swallowed. "I mean my—" This was going

to be harder than she thought. "Well, this weekend I went to have my palm read from one of these—see, I got this card on my birthday—"

"Oh, Julie!" Megan slapped her forehead. "How could I forget your birthday? I feel like such a stupe—why didn't you tell me? Two weeks ago I thought of it and then Charlie asked me to his sister's ballet recital and all I could think of was what I was going to wear and would his family like me and should I wear flats or heels and . . . oh, man, Julie—I'm sorry. Are you really, really mad at me?" Before Julie could answer, Megan brightened. "I know just what I'm going to get you." She patted Julie's hand. "You'll absolutely love it."

Julie sighed. It didn't make a particle of difference what Megan gave her. Her life was not about lipstick and fingernail polish. The bell rang. Julie grabbed her books and hurried off to class.

All day long Julie thought about being Jewel Young. It felt absolutely amazing. She wanted to jump on top of her desk and start tap dancing and pull all the flags off the bulletin board and stick them in her hair and yell, "Look, everyone—I'm Jewel Young!" She felt if she didn't hold onto the bottom of her chair seat she would start spinning like a top through every class, down the hall, out the door, through all the streets of Canopy. To keep herself from thinking too hard about Loretta Young, Julie made herself concentrate on a dot of yellow chalk high up on the chalkboard, away from all the dates of the Revolutionary War. Besides the strange feelings that had taken over her body, strange things kept happening to her. Not once, but three times.

When Mr. Annelin called on her, she thought he had said, "Jewel, do you know the answer?" She was so startled she just stared at him. "Julie, did you hear me?" After he repeated the question she thought maybe he had said, "Jule"—like the beginning of her name. But she didn't think so. It was Jewel. She was sure of that.

Then there was the question he asked her. "How long after we left the mother country did we adopt a new constitution?" It was just like, "How long after you left your mother were you adopted?" It gave her the shivers all day long.

And then, as Julie was walking down the hall to leave school, a boy came up behind her and put his hands over her eyes. When she turned around, he got red in the face. "Sorry," he said. "I thought you were someone else." Julie just stood there, staring after him, wondering how he had known that she *was* someone else. It was a miracle, she thought.

But at the end of the day something even more amazing happened. Her father had picked her up at Springhill, where she had played "I'm from Borneo," so many times that all the old people got up and left. When Julie got home she still couldn't settle down. She couldn't study. She couldn't sleep. All she could think about was how Loretta gave her away and then came back for her. She went to her desk and wrote a song in one big flurry of inspiration. Then she sat on her bed and sang it:

Homeless and orphaned and thrown out on her own
The beautiful maiden was heavy with child.
Tortured and hungry and oh, so alone
She gave birth to her baby way out in the wild.

Poverty forced her to give away her jewel,
She wandered in heartache all over the land,
For over ten years she felt just like a fool,
Until her lost jewel before her did stand.

Lost baby, lost baby, before her did stand.
Lost jewel, lost jewel, again in her hand.

She put her pajamas on, singing the words over and over. It was a perfect song. Her best ever. "Lost baby—" she sang as she turned out the light. Suddenly she remembered something that made her sit right up in bed. Loretta Young had another baby named Bagley Wonder. Julie had a baby brother.

5

Julie found that lying to Mrs. Wigmore was easier the second time. "My finger is still swollen," she said. "It's like a sausage. The doctor said another two weeks before I can play again."

Mrs. Wigmore clucked sympathetically and told Julie to keep up in her theory workbook. She would see her in two weeks. That was all. Mrs. Wigmore had actually believed her, Julie thought, clutching her piano books against her chest and hanging on to the aisle pole with her other hand. She had decided to stand on the bus so she wouldn't get stuck next to Beer Breath again—or somebody worse.

When the driver called out, "Penny Lane," Julie was off the bus in seconds, heading straight for the big, white house. She barely glanced at the guy working under his hood, still banging away as if he hadn't budged since last week. The sidewalks hadn't been shoveled and she could feel snow crunching around inside her loafers. Stopping, she balanced on her left foot to shake the snow out of her right shoe. All of a sudden, she saw the big black dog leap across Loretta Young's yard and barrel toward her like a locomotive.

"No!" She dropped her shoe and her music books and ran back in the direction she had come. "Help!" she yelled, stumbling through the gray drifts of snow. "Someone help me!"

She ran around the yellow-and-black car and crouched behind the man just as the dog leaped at her. The man reached out, caught him by his silver collar, and flipped him to the pavement. Then he bent over and stuck his finger down into the dog's face and held it there like he was giving him a stern warning about his behavior. But when he stood up and turned to Julie he was smiling broadly, as if the whole thing was a joke.

She wasn't in a smiley mood. "That horrible, vicious dog—he tried to kill me! You should call the dog pound on him. Did you see him attack me?"

The man, who was in his early twenties, pulled the bandanna off his head and rubbed his hands on it, taking his time. He looked her up and down. Then he laughed, which made Julie want to kick him in the shins. "You're a regular firecracker, aren't you, tootie?" Holding the bottom of his grimy jacket down with one hand, he reached into his pocket with the other and pulled out a dog biscuit. "Here, Winston." The dog pounced as if he hadn't eaten in a year and started crunching the biscuit between his big teeth. "Here—" He pulled out another biscuit and offered it to Julie.

"No thanks," she said sarcastically.

"Go on," he said. "Throw this to Winston and he'll be your pal forever."

She pointed at the dog. "If that—that—dog was the last living thing on earth I wouldn't have him for a friend." But she took the dog biscuit and shoved it in her pocket. Taking a hard look at Winston, who was still crunching away, she started off again toward the big, white house.

"Hey—tootie, what's your name?" he called after her.

"Jewel," she called over her shoulder, feeling a little shiver of delight.

"I'm Ike."

When she was halfway up the street, he yelled again. "Hey, Jewel—ask Loretta if there's a pair of shoes in your future."

She could hear his laughter ringing in the air behind her. "Jerk," she muttered. When she got back to her shoe, her foot was so cold it ached. She snatched her piano books out of the snow and crammed on her shoe, scooping up snow as she did it. "Crud on a crutch," she said, stomping angrily toward the white house.

Mrs. Og opened the door. "Dere you are, Sveetface," she said, breaking into a smile. She drew Julie inside and took her face in her hands. "Ach, such icy cheeks."

The touch of Mrs. Og's warm hands on her face was comforting and so was the smell of cinnamon that came from her apron. Julie smiled back and allowed Mrs. Og to help her off with her coat. When she kicked off her shoes, Mrs. Og looked at her socks and put a hand to her chest.

"You valk in da snow vitout your shoes?" Not waiting for an answer, she pulled Julie into the big living room where Loretta Young was seated at the long table talking into one of the black phones. She jumped up and leaned over the table, wiggling her fingers at Julie.

"Sit, Jewel," instructed Mrs. Og. "I bring you sometink."

Julie sank into a beanbag chair and tucked her cold, wet foot underneath her. It was like sitting on a block of ice.

"Now that was a mistake," Loretta Young said into the phone, dropping back into her chair. "You've got to stay asleep, even if you're scared, see. Just let yourself slide and land and see what fascinating things are down there. And next time, try swimming, see? Don't worry about a thing," she said earnestly. "It'll be hunky-dory." She cradled the phone against her shoulder and made paddling motions in the air.

Mrs. Og hurried in from a back hallway holding a thick pair of gray wool socks. "Your feet, Sugar," she said.

Julie hesitated. "Umm, whose socks are those?"

"Silly goose." Mrs. Og bent down and pulled off Julie's wet socks.

She tried not to imagine that the strange man named Cramp had worn these socks. Yet, they were so warm it was like stepping into hot chocolate. "Thank you," she said to Mrs. Og. But she was looking at Loretta Young, who was still talking on the phone and plucking at the chain of gold stars around her neck.

"On the other hand," she was saying, "you shouldn't get all hyped up or you'll lose it entirely. You'll flat wake up." As Loretta talked, her gold star earrings swung around and around in delicate little circles, like tiny orbits. This woman with the bright yellow hair and gold stars was her mother, Julie thought, the missing piece to Julie's whole life. After all these years she was there right in front of her, close enough to touch. All the questions Julie had carried in her heart, Loretta could answer. Loretta and only Loretta, she thought, could make her whole. Normal. Like everybody else. The thought of it was so exciting, Julie couldn't sit still. She jumped out of the beanbag and walked back and forth across the room.

"There," Loretta said, hanging up the phone and smiling a wide, red smile at Julie. "You know what? That was better than a Walt Disney movie. Feature this—a giant slide all the way from the Milky Way right down to the bottom of the Atlantic Ocean." She traced a long arc through the air. "Isn't that a flitter?"

Julie smiled back, not at all sure what Loretta was talking about.

Loretta got up and looped her arm through Julie's. "We're going to have a party. We're going to celebrate all day long."

Julie stiffened. They had barely said hello and already she was going to disappoint Loretta. "Umm, I can only stay about an hour," she murmured, searching Loretta's face for signs of rejection.

Loretta laughed. "Are you having your piano lesson again?"

Julie nodded. "See—I was going to tell my mother that you—that I—I mean, I wanted her to know but I thought maybe it might be a little hard for her. She's kind of old and—"

"She'd have a conniption fit," Loretta said.

Julie nodded.

"What she doesn't know won't hurt her," Loretta said decisively. "C'mon, I got a surprise for you." She led Julie into the room where Mrs. Og had gone. "In here."

It was a huge kitchen with faded black-and-white tiles on the floor and white, painted cupboards that went all the way up to the tall ceiling. A big stove stood on short, metal legs, looking like something from an old advertisement for Campbell Soup. Dozens of little windows set in two of the walls allowed sunlight to pour over everything in the room. And in the center of the kitchen was a battered oak table with claw feet big enough to seat ten or twelve people. On the table stood a remarkable cake. It was a castle, frosted in pink, with towers and gates and chocolate windows and fourteen cannons made from caramels, with Life Savers wheels and candles laid across as barrels. At the top of the tower was a small flag on which someone had written, *Happy Birthday, Jewel.*

Julie couldn't believe her eyes. Loretta Young had been thinking about her, expecting her. She had baked her the most beautiful cake in the world. "That cake," she whispered, not trusting her voice, "that is the most beautiful cake I've ever seen. Ever."

"Oh, I know it," Loretta agreed. "Mrs. Og baked it." She pointed at Mrs. Og, who was stirring cookie batter at the counter. "But that's not the surprise. Here's the surprise." She stepped to a door just beyond the end of the table and knocked. "Ready?"

A shuffling noise came from the other side and then the door flew open. Out came a small, white-haired boy with large glasses. He was in a wheelchair. "Wow," he said, looking at Julie out of wide, gray eyes.

Her eyes flicked down to his thin, little legs and then back to his face. "Um, hi."

"Are you my sister? Are you Jewel?" the boy asked.

Julie blinked. She turned to Loretta.

"It's Bagley," Loretta said, nodding eagerly. "Like I told you? Bagley Wonder."

"O-o-h," Julie said. "Oh, I thought—"

"You thought I could walk," Bagley said cheerfully. "Didn't you?"

Julie blushed. "I thought you were a baby. You said" —she turned to Loretta— "you said your baby—" She was mortified. Why didn't she just keep her big mouth shut?

"I'm ten," Bagley said. "But I'm small for my age. She still calls me her baby. Do you wish I was a baby?"

"Oh, no," Julie said. She started snapping her rubber band. "Oh, no," she repeated, staring at Bagley. He *was* small, as small as a seven-year-old and his skin was so pale you could see the veins in his forehead. He was blond but not the same blond as Loretta and Julie. He had the white hair of a very old man. In fact, he looked a lot like a frail, old man, with fragile limbs and a pale, bony face. He looked breakable. But, under his glasses, his gray eyes were alert and they looked directly into Julie's. There was nothing timid in the look. Being in a wheelchair was not something to apologize for.

Julie tried not to but she glanced at his legs again. Except for the muscular dystrophy poster child, she had never seen a little kid in a wheelchair. "I think you're—you're just fine." She sucked in her breath. He was so little, she thought, and so white and so pretty. No—so delicate. He reminded her of an angel—a little angel in a wheelchair.

Her entire life Julie had dreamed of having a little sister or brother, somebody to piggyback around the yard, to tell ghost stories to. She used to hold Jacquelina tight and pray that she would come alive in the night while she slept. Now Bagley was the answer to her prayers. He was a real, live little brother.

"Bagley Wonder," she said out loud. Then, because it felt stupid to just say his name, she added, "I like your T-shirt." It said, STARFISHER. "I play that song on the piano a lot. For the old people at the nursing home."

"Wow! Do you play the piano? Would you play that song for me?"

One of the phones rang in the other room. "Mrs. Og, can you get that?" Loretta said over her shoulder. "If it's Nellie or The Dancing Man, I'll come." She turned back to Julie. "Some people will only discuss their dreams with me, you know? But Mrs. Og is swell. Not Cramp—he's definitely small beer. On a good day he can only hang on to someone for three minutes. Thanks, Oggie," she yelled as Mrs. Og disappeared down the hallway.

Dreams? Julie thought, wondering if people called Loretta just to discuss their dreams. Why in the world would people want to talk about their dreams?

"The thing about dreams," Loretta said, as if she had been reading Julie's mind, "is this: They're movies of our feelings, but like in a code. Take milk, for instance. Dreaming about drinking milk means good health and prosperity. Goat's milk means good luck in your job. But say, spilled milk? Watch out. If you're not extra careful, you're gonna be in some deep trouble. See, it all depends. Like, do you ever dream of milk?"

Julie was so astonished at having Loretta read her mind that she couldn't answer. She pushed up her glasses and stared at her.

"Ma—the presents," Bagley said impatiently.

"There's a lot more to this," Loretta said, unwrapping a piece of gum. "I'll go over it with you some time. You oughta know about dreams." She bent down and opened the oven door where the presents were stashed.

"Wait, wait," Bagley said, waving his hands. "Close your eyes."

Julie shut her eyes. She saw Bagley in his wheelchair floating on the inside of her eyelids, and Loretta Young smiling her bright, red smile. Her brother and her mother, she thought, her insides melting with joy.

When she opened them, would they disappear? Was this a dream like the lady who slid down the Milky Way into the Atlantic Ocean? The thick wool socks picked at her feet. Smells of cinnamon and fried onions rose to her nostrils. A faucet dripped, a clock ticked. In the next room, she heard a singsong voice saying, "Dere you have it. The seaveed means someone's going to have a party." Julie felt dizzy.

"Open your eyes!"

Bagley was holding out a big, triangle-shaped kite. Julie took it and turned it over, running her fingers over the neatly glued edges, the carefully painted stripes. She looked at him. "Did you make this?"

"Yes! It's my deluxe turbo delta. I make all kinds—hearts on a string, dragons, diamonds. I love kites. I love anything that flies."

"This is so neat," she said. "Thanks, Bagley." She wondered if she should ask him to fly it with her sometime. But could people in wheelchairs do things like that? Maybe he wasn't even allowed to go outside. "It's the best," she said.

"This is from me," Loretta Young said, handing her a box wrapped in the comics section of the newspaper. It was a home permanent. Julie looked at Loretta to see if it was a joke. "Sometime I'll give you a perm," Loretta said. "I'm a hair stylist too—a great one." She flipped her curls back with her hand. "Who do you think did mine?"

"Gee, thanks," Julie said. "Nobody ever gave me a perm before."

"I could tell," Loretta said. "Well, we'd better cut the cake." She stepped into the doorway. "Mrs. Og! Cramp! We're cutting the cake."

Loretta handed Bagley the matches and Julie a long knife. "I'll get the coffee," she said.

Bagley wheeled up to the table. He pulled out a match and struck it against the back of the matchbook. Julie caught her breath, wanting to stop him. Her mother wouldn't let her use matches at fourteen, let alone ten. But Bagley was fearless; he lit all the candles on one match, his small hand as quick as lightning.

While Julie sat before the glowing cake, they sat around the table and sang—Loretta and Bagley, Mrs. Og, and the man with the ponytail named Cramp. Their voices all stuck out at different angles—Bagley's high as a chickadee, Mrs. Og's with her strange way of pronouncing words, Cramp's as deep as a bullfrog, and Loretta's bright and twangy. It reminded Julie of when she played at Springhill and the old people sang. It was as if they were all singing different songs. But, to her, it was the most beautiful song she'd ever heard.

Loretta poured coffee for everyone, even Bagley. Julie cut five pieces and put them on the five plates Loretta had taken down from the cupboard. The plates were chipped and old, Julie noticed, but they looked festive under the pink cake with its load of caramel cannons and bright Life Savers wheels. And, for the first time, Julie drank coffee, black—like Loretta—sucking it through the cake to take away the bitterness.

"Did you make a wish?" Bagley asked.

Julie nodded. "I wish that I can come to Dreamland forever."

6

All her life, Julie knew she was different. She hated doing the things her parents loved to do and loved doing what made her parents cringe. Once, when she was five, the minister of the Canopy Community Presbyterian Church gathered all the children around him on the altar so he could tell them the story of the angel who came down to tell Mary she was going to have Baby Jesus. Julie had heard the story before and she hadn't found it that interesting the first time. What was interesting was being on the altar looking out at a crowd of dressed-up people all looking back at her. She stood up straight and started to sing: "Old Sweetlips, my porker, my little hambone—" It was her favorite song.

"I—" said her mother, pressing her hands to her huge bosom every time she told the story, "have never been so embarrassed in my entire life." But she had. Lots of times after that. Mame and Wayne Solus always expected a small, blond version of themselves—someone prim, modest, and good tempered, who always said excuse me when she burped and never knocked over chairs to get to the telephone. But Julie didn't have their virtues any more than she had their blood running through her veins. For her, being adopted was the most mortifying thing of all. Because she wasn't like anybody—not Wayne and Mame, not like all her friends who knew where the color of their eyes came from or the shape of their noses. For fourteen years she had looked in the mirror and seen a strange person with gray eyes and a long, skinny nose. A stranger, even to herself.

But Loretta had changed all that, she thought giddily. She set down the cup of coffee she had been drinking and slid her fingers along the keyboard, singing in her sultriest Etta Jonas voice:

Homeless and orphaned and thrown out on her own
The beautiful maiden was heavy with child.
Tortured and hungry and oh, so alone
She gave birth—

"What's this?" Her mother appeared, holding a dog biscuit.

"Where did you get that?" Julie sat up and stared, as if she had never seen it before.

"It was in your coat pocket, that's where it was. What is a dog biscuit doing in your coat?"

"Oh." Julie nodded. "Oh, a dog biscuit. It's for this dog—" She sifted through her brain for an explanation. "At school," she went on. "Everyone gives him dog biscuits."

"Is this a stray dog?" her mother asked, pointing the biscuit at Julie accusingly. "The truth, Julie."

Julie shook her head. "Uh-uh. It belongs to this boy." She started singing again—one of the Springhill songs. "You can get away from Harry, you can get away from Larry—"

"And where did you get that cup of coffee?"

She groaned. "It was Dad's. He didn't finish it."

Her mother whisked it away. "Children don't drink coffee, Julie. It will stunt your growth."

Julie looked over her shoulder as her mother's enormous behind disappeared into the kitchen. "Well, it didn't stunt yours," she muttered, turning back to the keyboard.

Mrs. Solus stuck her head back in. "I'm frying you some turkey bacon, dear. I don't think you're getting enough protein."

"That's just hunky-dory," she called back. "That's the hunkiest of the doriest." She liked the expressions Loretta Young used. They were different from the same old tired phrases her parents used. She started playing "You Can Get Away from Harry," and singing, "You can get away from Hunky, you can get away from Dory, you can get away from Hunky, but you can't get away from—"

Her mother came back in again. "I saw Mrs. Wigmore yesterday."

Julie caught her breath and snatched her fingers off the keyboard. Mrs. Wigmore had asked how Julie's sprained finger was and when she would return to her lessons. Of course, of course, it was bound to happen, she thought. She was a filthy liar. She would never be trusted again. Never, ever, would she be allowed to show her face at Mrs. Wigmore's again.

"But she was way over in the hanging baskets at English Gardens so I didn't get a chance to say hello."

Julie let out her breath. "Is my bacon ready?" she asked, getting up from the bench.

At the breakfast table, Julie examined the gold-bordered plates. She tapped one with her finger. "Are we rich?"

"Damn right," her father said, behind his paper.

"Wayne!" her mother said. "Of course we aren't rich, Julie. What a question. The Rockefellers are rich. The Hearsts are rich. We're just—I'd say, we're comfortable."

"Like how much did these plates cost?" She lifted the plate and examined the bottom. "Haviland," she read. "And what about those other plates—the company ones with the painted flowers?"

Her father looked up from his paper. "Are you getting married?"

She made a face at him and appealed to her mother. "Most people can't afford stuff like this, right?"

Her mother set Julie's vitamins on her plate and poured her husband another cup of coffee. "Darling, when you get married—and that will be eons from now—all this will be yours. And, of course, you have all of Grandma's things in your hope chest down in the basement."

Julie shook her head. She didn't want her mother's plates or any of the boxes and boxes of china and statues and crystal they had brought home when Grandma moved into a nursing home. She just wondered why her own mother and her own brother had to eat off cracked plates when she—their own flesh and blood—ate off expensive china. She reached over and took a sip of her father's coffee without his noticing. "Did you ever think—" she began, "that we have enough dishes to serve sixty people, maybe a hundred people. I mean, here we are, three people in this huge house with plates coming out of our ears. That's a waste. It's criminal."

Her mother sighed as she returned to the table. "Julie, if I thought for a minute that I could improve the lot of another family by giving away my china I would. But, darling, it's hardly a crime. Your father bought me the tulip service and Aunt Juliana left—"

"She's the one." Julie put down her vitamin C tablet. "Is she the one I'm named after?"

Her mother nodded. "Juliana Blanche Snoudy."

Julie took another swallow of her father's coffee. No one seemed to notice. Her father was buried in the stock market and her mother was reading about the missing children on the milk carton as she did every morning. "I've been thinking," she said slowly, pouring more cream in her father's cup, "didn't my—my birth mother give me a name? You know—just for the birth certificate or something?"

Her mother laughed, more of a snort, really, and put the milk carton down. "Now why on earth would you ask a question like that?"

"Just wondering," Julie mumbled, immediately feeling guilty. Whenever she tried to find out anything about her adoption, her mother always made Julie feel terrible, like she was being unforgivably rude. Over the years she had learned not to ask at all. But suddenly that policy didn't seem fair. "What's so bad about asking that," Julie said, tracing the gold rim of the plate with her finger.

"Water over the dam, Julie," her father said. "Who can remember what happened yesterday, let alone the Dark Ages."

"You call fourteen years ago the Dark Ages!"

Her father put his paper down and looked at her. "Sticky wicket," he said.

"Sticky wicket," Julie repeated later as she pulled on her headphones. She and Jacquelina were sitting in the window seat, staring out at the Big Dipper hanging over the swimming pool. "Sticky wicket" is what her father always said when he wanted her to drop something. He acted as if her mother's feelings were too delicate to tell Julie the simple fact about whether or not her birth mother had given her a name. She couldn't understand why her parents couldn't just level with her.

For as long as Julie could remember, they had told her she was adopted, but as she got older and started to ask questions about what her real mother and father were like, they acted like she was prying into their personal business. Her father would start busying himself with his dental journals, reading aloud about the four stages of periodontal disease as if he could distract her from the subject. And, if anything, her mother was worse. When Julie was little she fed her a schmaltzy story about her mother being a pink fairy with cotton candy hair and silver wings. The updated version was this: "Though we didn't know her we knew she was a beautiful person because she gave us you." It was all sweetness and joy.

And that, Julie thought, was how they wanted her to consider her adoption. She went from being the daughter of a poor, but lovable young woman to being the daughter of a rich, but adoring, middle-aged couple. Simple and sweet and perfect. They never admitted to any confusion or pain. So how could she?

Julie pulled Jacquelina onto her lap and thought about what was happening to her. What would her parents think if they knew she had actually visited with her mother—with Loretta Young—actually celebrated her birthday with her? And what would they say if they knew she had a little brother who liked her a lot. And they wanted her to come back. Loretta and Bagley both said they wanted her to come back.

Julie thought about going to visit Loretta and Bagley every week for one hour. It was hopeless. Laying her cheek against Jacquelina's cool face she thought how impossible it would be to keep lying about her finger. Besides, one hour was just barely enough time to take her coat off and have a cup of coffee. She had a thousand questions to ask Loretta.

Julie had to figure out a way not to have to go to her father's office after her piano lesson on Saturdays. It was so stupid to go there just because her mother had to go up to Griffinville every weekend to visit Grandma Snoudy. It had been Julie's mother's idea, anyway, not hers. Since she was away, she decided it was the perfect opportunity for Julie and her father to spend some time together. The reality was not nearly so cozy. Mr. Solus—Dr. Solus—spent the day poking around in patients' mouths and his conversation was limited to asking questions about flossing and brushing. He was glad to have Julie around but he didn't consider this as father-daughter time any more than she did.

Julie dragged Jacquelina over on the bed next to her and lay there staring at the ceiling. If only she could just say it. "I would like to visit my birth mother on Saturdays." She tried to imagine her mother saying, "What a lovely idea, dear. And why not take along these pretty earrings? I know how much Loretta likes jewelry. Remember not to stare at Bagley's wheelchair, darling. He's a normal little boy with feelings just like you and me. Wouldn't you like to take them this pot of violets?" She heaved a great sigh. Never in a million years would her mother encourage her to visit Loretta Young. Even if it was the most important thing in the world to Julie.

"It is," Julie whispered to Jacquelina. "It's absolutely the most important thing in the world." She took off Jacquelina's scarf and draped it over her own face.

"Julie, why on earth was this pinned into that silly mannequin's hair?" Her mother's voice startled her awake. Julie pulled the scarf from her face. Her mother was holding the brooch Julie's father had given her.

"Oh," she said, "I was just fooling around."

"This isn't a dimestore bauble," her mother said, setting it on the dresser. "If you aren't going to wear it, put it in your jewelry box. Here, I brought you some hot chocolate."

When Julie's mother sat on the bed, her weight made Julie roll toward her. She pushed herself back and hung onto the headboard so she wouldn't slide back to her mother. "Geeze—" she said, looking at the clock on her dresser. "I slept for an hour and a half. I still have two chapters in American Government to read."

Her mother leaned over and hugged her. "Good little Julie."

Julie stiffened. "You know, I'm not exactly in diapers, Mom. I'll be driving a car in two more years."

Her mother waved the idea away. "Oh, goodness, that's ages and ages down the road. Don't rush yourself into old age. Besides, you're still my baby." She squeezed Julie tighter.

"Mom—" Julie pulled away. "Listen, Mom, I hate staying at Dad's office on Saturdays. He doesn't really need me and I'm just in the way."

"Well, then, you can just come with me and visit Grandma Snoudy."

Julie jumped off the bed. "I knew you were going to say that—I just knew it! I hate seeing Grandma Snoudy. She's—she's strange."

Her mother looked crushed. "You know your grandmother adores you, Julie. Why I bet she would perk right up if you came to Whispering Meadows and started playing 'The Surrey with the Fringe on Top.'"

" 'Surrey with the Fringe on Top?' Mom, she doesn't even remember who I am. I don't exactly want to go see someone who calls me a different name every week." She looked at her mother's wounded face. "Once in a while, maybe," she added.

Julie's mother stood up. She reached out and tucked Julie's hair behind her ears. "I'm not going to force you. That's why we agreed that you don't have to go to Griffinville, that it's fine to spend Saturdays at your father's office while I'm gone."

Julie wanted to scream. Her mother had a way of sounding reasonable, as if Julie had the ability to chose for herself. But the choices weren't Julie's choices. They were her mother's. "I don't want to go to Dad's office and I don't want to go to Griffinville to see Grandma. I just want to go home after my piano lesson."

"By yourself?" It was the same tone of voice she used when she read them the milk cartons in the morning. "Anything can happen. I read of a young girl being snatched from her bed through an open window."

"An open window? Mom, it's February."

"Out of the question." Her mother crossed her arms over her chest and shook her head.

Julie saw all her hopes dashed. What was the point, she thought, of finding Loretta and Bagley if she could never see them? What was the point in even knowing they existed? They might as well be on Venus. It wasn't fair. She could be with her senile old grandmother any day of the week, but being with Bagley and Loretta was way more important. They were family in a way Grandma Snoudy could never be. "No!" Julie yelled. "I won't go to Dad's office! I'm fourteen years old—I can take care of myself!"

"Now, sweetheart—" Her mother reached out to smooth her hair again but Julie pulled away.

"Just stop trying to plan my whole life!" Julie picked up a magazine and threw it against the wall. "I can't walk to the corner without you breathing down my neck. You won't even let me light the candles on my own cake. You're a big, wet blanket." Julie stalked out of the room, slamming the door on her mother. She ran down the hall and bumped into her father, who was coming out of the bathroom after his foot soak. "She ruins everything," Julie wailed to her father.

Mr. Solus looked from Julie to his wife who had followed Julie, red-faced, out of the room. "Julie," he said warningly. Then, looking at Mame, he said in a softer voice, "Are you all right, Mother?"

"Not her," Julie yelled. She thumped her chest. "Me. Me."

She took a deep breath. How could she explain that she had been lost for fourteen years and now she was found? That finally, finally, her life was beginning to make sense because she knew who she was. That it didn't matter anymore about her gray eyes and skinny nose. That it didn't matter about feeling like an apple core. She wasn't an apple core anymore. The person who gave her away had come back for her. Julie wanted desperately to say these things to her mother and father, to share the miracle that had transformed her life. But, even in her anger, she wanted not to hurt them. So she just yelled the things she always yelled.

"You don't trust me. I'm fourteen years old and you don't trust me. I have to go to your stupid office every Saturday like a three-year-old because you and Mom don't trust me."

"Aah, Julie, we do trust you. Your mother and I have every confidence in your ability to look after yourself for a day, even an entire weekend. But," he looked at Mame pointedly, "your mother doesn't trust the rest of the world. She's afraid the bogeyman will get you."

"It's not fair." Julie leaned against the wall and groaned loudly. "You treat me like a child. Every other fourteen-year-old I know gets to stay alone. Avery Gully stays alone every afternoon for three hours until her mom gets home from work and Megan Ward baby-sits for her sister all day Saturdays. She's the same age I am and her parents trust her to take care of herself *and* Holly. It's not fair," she said again, directing her complaints to her father who, she sensed, was more sympathetic.

There was a long silence. Her father took the towel from around his neck, bent over and patted his feet. He stood up and looked at Mame again.

"No," she said. "Fourteen is too young to stay alone."

Julie suddenly pushed herself from the wall. "Wait a minute, wait a minute. I could go there—to Megan's, while she's baby-sitting. She'd love it. I know she would."

Her father looked at her mother. "Would that do?"

Mrs. Solus looked from her husband to Julie, her face tense and humorless. "I know you think I'm an old worrywart," she said, pressing her fingers to her temples. "I read things. Every day I read about children being abducted from their homes, their schoolyards. Those parents—how do they go on after that? How do they get up in the morning, knowing their most precious gift is missing? Am I so foolish," she asked, her voice getting shriller, "to want to protect my daughter from that kind of danger?"

Julie shrugged her shoulders. She had heard it all before. Mame then looked at her husband. "Is this all right, Wayne? Will she be safe over there?"

He took her hand and gave it a pat. "This will be fine, Mame. I think we should give our permission."

7

Julie carried her Harrod's bag in one hand and a bag from Wong Lee's in the other. It hadn't snowed all week and the sun reflected brightly off the hard-crusted surfaces in both directions along Penny Lane. Down by the box houses a dozen little kids were sliding down a snowbank, taking turns on a sheet of red plastic. Julie could hear their laughter over the grinding gears of the departing bus. She stepped away from the curb and looked over at the café.

"Hey, Jewel."

She wiggled the fingers of one hand at Ike, who was standing in the doorway of the restaurant. His car, apparently fixed, was parked next to the restaurant with the hood closed. Gone were the grimy jacket and bandanna; he was wearing clean khakis and a white apron. Julie wondered if he worked there, though it didn't look like they ever had any business. The drab green shutters were crooked and the sign over the door read, OD FOOD. No wonder there wasn't any business, she thought, grinning. Who wanted to eat odd food?

As soon as she saw Winston charging down the street Julie wanted to scream. But she didn't. Instead she set down the Chinese food and grabbed two dog biscuits out of her Harrod's bag. When Winston was within leaping distance she threw them. They sailed across the crusty snow like hockey pucks. Winston pounced, attacking them like a jungle beast. Pleased with herself, Julie gave the dog a wide berth and headed up the street to the big house, sinking through the crusty snow with every step.

This time, Loretta opened the door and when she saw Julie coming up the walk, her face broke into a huge smile. "Look who's walkin' up the sidewalk, see who's strollin' down the stree—eet," she sang, holding her hands over her head and doing a shimmy in a tight, red miniskirt.

Julie was glad she had worn the red beret that Megan had finally given her for her birthday. It made her feel kind of jazzy, Loretta Youngish. She smiled back and held out the Chinese food. "From my mother."

Loretta's mouth dropped open. "No bull?"

Julie laughed as she came inside. "Well, not exactly." She waved at Mrs. Og who went by wearing oven mitts. Looking around for Bagley, she dropped her coat on the beanbag. "See, my mother has to go to Griffinville to visit my grandma, and my dad works Saturdays so she ordered from Wong Lee's for me and my girlfriend."

"Ha!" Loretta said. "I bet she doesn't know the girlfriend is me." She took the box and clicked off to the kitchen on her red high heels. "This stuff smells fab. Be sure and thank her for me. Ha ha." She shoved aside two pies that were cooling on the counter and set down the bag of egg rolls. Then she picked up a wad of gum stuck to a plate and popped it in her mouth. "You gonna start going off weekends to visit your grandma?"

"Just my mom goes," Julie said.

Loretta whirled around and clapped her hands. "You can stay all day?"

Julie nodded. "I just have to make a credit card call if it's okay? To my mom, to let her know I'm here—I mean, at my friend's house."

Loretta winked. "You're a smart cookie, Jewel." She laughed. "Course, you come by it naturally." The phone rang and Loretta motioned for Julie to follow her into the living room.

While Loretta answered the phone, Julie picked up another line to call her mother. "I'm here," she said brightly, "at Megan's." Then she hung up and slumped down into the chair next to Loretta, suddenly feeling like a worm.

Loretta hung up and spun around in her chair to face Julie. "So," she said cheerily, "you're visiting a girlfriend, is that the story?"

"Yeah," Julie said glumly.

"What's wrong?" Loretta lifted her hands in the air. "Didn't she believe you?"

"Oh, she believed me," Julie said. "I set this up like a master criminal. First, I called my friend, Megan, and asked if I could pretend to visit her every Saturday because I was going somewhere else. And Megan said that was perfect because her boyfriend sneaks over every Saturday while she's baby-sitting and now she thinks I'm sneaking off to visit a boyfriend every Saturday, too. And my mom thinks I'm going over to help Megan baby-sit every Saturday. So I lied to Megan and I lied to my mother. But everything is just hunky-dory."

"Well, of course it is," Loretta said reassuringly. "You're just not used to lying, that's all." She stood up and put both hands on Julie's shoulders. "But look, Jewel, is there any other way you could get over here every Saturday? Like, say—" She raised her voice several octaves, "By the way, folks, I'm going to visit my real mother today. Okey-dokey?"

Julie laughed and shook her head.

"There you are. You got no choice in the matter." The phone rang again; Loretta plunked herself down on the table top to answer it.

Julie thought about what Loretta had said. There was no way she could tell her parents where she went on Saturdays. If lying was the only way she could get here, then she had to do it. She looked at

Loretta sitting on top of the table in her red miniskirt. Finally, she had all the time in the world to get the answers to her questions.

"You watch your mailbox," Loretta was saying into the phone. "I'll bet you'll be getting it by Tuesday for certain. If not this Tuesday, then next Tuesday. And hon—it might help if you sleep on your left side. Okay? Bye, now. Keep in touch." She hung up and looked at Julie. "That Nellie—she's worth twenty-five dollars every time she calls."

Julie blinked. "People pay you that much to talk about dreams?"

"Sure, five dollars a minute times five minutes." Loretta popped her gum. "Listen, we better get started on that perm."

"Perm?" Julie's mouth dropped open. "But I wanted to talk."

"Now don't look so pickled, Jewel. Do you want hair like a prairie dog? Trust me, a good head of curl will turn you into a regular confection." She reached into a drawer under the table and pulled out the home permanent Julie had left behind from her birthday celebration. "Besides," Loretta said, tapping the box with her fingernails, "perms are the best excuses in the world to talk. We'll talk till we're blue in the face. Me and you and Bagley"—she paused and looked around— "when he gets back upstairs. We'll just get cozy while we do you up." She handed Julie the perm. "First, some coffee."

Loretta was combing Julie's hair when Bagley rolled in with a box of donuts. "Jewel," he yelled and rolled over to the stool she was sitting on.

Julie hugged him, pressing her cheek against his. His face was warm and his hair was plastered against his forehead.

"Look at this, Jewel," he shouted. He pushed up his sleeve and made a muscle with his skinny little arm.

She felt it. "Wow, Popeye. Have you been lifting weights?"

He nodded. "Down in the basement. In Cramp's gym."

He took four jelly beans out of his pocket and dropped them, one at a time in his mouth. "He's going to build me up until I'm as big as he is. He used to be a boxer." He threw a couple of punches in the air. "Did you miss me, Jewel?"

"I sure did," she said, looking into his earnest little face. "I missed you like the night misses the moon. Like the cat misses the mouse. Like, umm . . ."

"Like the kite misses the wind." He rocked with laughter.

"Okay, Bagley. Let her go. I gotta get rollin' here," Loretta said.

But before she had a chance to start, the phone rang again. Loretta always answered the same way. "Queen of Dreamland. Tell me about your dream."

Julie was annoyed. She wanted Loretta to stop everything and pay attention to her. "Why do people keep bothering her?" she asked Bagley.

"They want to understand their dreams," he whispered back.

"But why? I don't get this whole thing about dreams. I just don't get why people pay so much—"

Just then, another phone rang and Loretta Young pointed at Bagley. He picked it up. "The Queen of Dreamland will be right with you," he said in his high, thin voice. He put his hand over the receiver. "Could you get Mrs. Og, please," he said to Julie. "She's in the circus room."

"Where's—"

"Never mind, Jewel," Loretta hissed. She spoke into her phone. "Just one second, sir, while I research that last item." She put her hand over the receiver. "Bagley, you go," she said, waving him off. "Jewel, you just read this stuff—where is it now?" She pulled open a drawer and took out a four by six printed card. "Just read this and by the time you're done, Mrs. Og will be here."

"But I don't—"

"Don't give it another thought," Loretta said airily. "Just read the card. Here we go, sir," she said, speaking into her phone again. "It sounds to me like a sign of a forthcoming promotion. Are you in line for a step up?" She pressed the card into Julie's hand.

Julie took a deep breath. "Umm, hello, sir?"

"I am not a sir," a woman's voice said, "and I have been waiting a full sixty seconds on this line. Now what about my kangaroo dream?"

Julie felt her forehead break out in little prickles of sweat. "Umm," she said, "umm." She looked at the card. "Umm, before we begin, miss or madam," she read, "there are some elements I'd like you to think about. The deep unconscious metal system—I mean mental system," she went on, "which dominates dream impressions—I, I mean, expressions. It has its own way of processing information. This means—I mean, it does *not* mean, that our waking view is real and our sleeping view is not real."

"Well, just what *does* it mean?" the woman demanded.

Julie had no idea what it meant. The words on the card were all gibberish to her. She looked wildly at Loretta for help.

"Just keep reading," Loretta whispered, putting her hand over the receiver. "Real slow. Think—five dollars a minute, five dollars a minute."

Julie looked back at the card. "You see, we have our conscious system and our unconscious system. Conscious is for waking thoughts, unconscious is for dream thoughts." That part made a little sense to her. She continued, "The reality is that our waking thoughts will not allow our dream thoughts into its realm of experience. That is, the conscious mind sees the dream world as—"

"Are you sure you're the Queen of Dreamland?"

"Umm, well, I'm, I'm—you'd better listen to me," Julie stuttered. She lowered her voice, trying to sound like Loretta. "Did you know kangaroos can go either way? It's like dreaming about milk. Did you ever have a dream about spilled milk?"

Just then, Mrs. Og tapped her on the shoulder. Julie leaped up from the table and thrust the receiver into her hand. "It's about a kangaroo," she hissed.

Mrs. Og nodded, slid into the chair, and said to the woman in her sweet, understanding voice, "So, my dear, you are dreaming about kangaroos? Dat is very interesting indeed. I vill tell you about kangaroos but first, you must tell me, does dis kangaroo have a baby in its carry bag? Dat makes all da difference."

Loretta hung up and looked at Julie. "You did great, Jewel."

Julie wiped her forehead. "God, I was awful. I don't know anything about dreams."

"Psssh." Loretta waved her nails in the air. "There's a trick to everything. You just need a flair with people. And you got that—I can tell. After a while, you just ad lib. Kettle dreams, murder dreams, riding on camel dreams, I know them all."

"No way," Julie said. "It was horrible, having that woman expect me to tell her something. I hated it."

"Well, of course," Loretta said crisply, "if you don't want to help out." She picked up the perm and clicked off down the hallway.

"I tink she vants you to follow, Honeylamb." Mrs. Og had gotten off the phone with the kangaroo lady and pointed after Loretta Young. "Here," she said, handing Julie a blue notebook. "Loretta's Dream List. I stay and answer da phones now."

Julie took the notebook and the two bags she'd brought and went off down the hall, wondering why Loretta seemed mad at her, why this phone thing was such a big deal. The room they entered was like a huge Laundromat. There were three big washers and dryers, a deep, green laundry tub, and wire baskets on wheels. Instead of clothes, the baskets were full of boxes of macaroni and cheese and cans of Spam and bags of marshmallows. Coming down from the ceiling were big cupboards with more boxes and cans of food inside. Along the far wall was a small bed piled with pillows, and a big, metal office desk with an engraved nameplate on it: BAGLEY WONDER.

Bagley sat in his wheelchair at the desk, working on a red kite. "This is my bedroom," he announced. "If I get too cold, I turn on all the dryers at once. Are you too cold?"

Julie shook her head.

"This is also the pantry. Mrs. Og brings us dented cans from the Green Giant. Are you hungry?"

"I'm starving," she said. "And I brought egg rolls." She reached into the paper bag and brought out the cardboard carton. "And look what else I brought." Julie carefully reached into the Harrod's bag and lifted out six plates, handing them to Loretta, one by one.

"My God," Loretta said, holding a flowered plate up to the ceiling light and pinging it with her fingernail. "These are absolutely gorgeous. But your mother is going to murder you."

"Oh, no, she's not," Julie said. "These plates were given to me by my grandma. I can do whatever I like with them."

Julie and Loretta ate their egg rolls off the fancy plates while Bagley ate two raspberry-filled donuts.

"He's eating a terrible lunch," Julie told Loretta.

"Bagley, that's four donuts you've had so far," Loretta said in an exasperated voice. But any hope that Loretta was going to get him to eat something better disappeared in the next breath. "Here, help sort these rods." Loretta licked her fingers and plunked down a box overflowing with plastic curlers on the metal desk. "We don't want the biggest, we don't want the skinniest. This," she said, holding up a pink one. "The Amber Sloan look." She looked at Julie. "You know, that cardiac nurse on *Tender Kisses*."

Loretta sprayed Julie's hair all over with an old window cleaner bottle filled with water. They set up a kind of rhythm. Loretta would section a piece of Julie's hair, Julie would hand her a tissue and Bagley a curler. While Loretta rolled up her hair, she cracked her gum and talked about Dreamland.

"All my life I got these messages in dreams. For instance, this happened to me when I was seven. The night before my turtle died she came to me in a dream like an angel, with big wings. 'Chow,' she goes to me. That's good-bye in Italian. And the next day she got hit by a Budweiser truck. I knew I would go into dreams sometime. Someplace." She snapped a curler tight up against Julie's neck. "Hey, I didn't mean to get cheesed off at you, Jewel. About the phone, ya know? Except we need the business."

"Every phone call helps," Bagley said, holding up a curler. "Five dollars a minute, five dollars a minute." He grinned at Julie, showing perfect little teeth. "We're poor."

"Really?" She turned to Loretta. "You are?"

Loretta pushed Julie's head back in position and snatched another tissue. "We aren't starving if that's what you're thinking. And we have a roof over our heads thanks to Cramp, who only charges us two hundred dollars and housecleaning, except for the gym in the basement, which Mrs. Og cleans because I can't hear the phones down there. But I own the business. I own Dreamland. Five dollars a minute for dreams, ten dollars to have your palm read. It's not what you'd call a pot of gold. Like, there's no money for Chinese carryout."

Julie winced but Loretta didn't notice. She sectioned off another piece of Julie's hair and wound it up tight. "You know how you wake up and you've been dreaming and your dream is right there in the room with you, bigger than life with seventeen actors in costume, mountains, sunsets, Charlton Heston, the works. And then, ten seconds later—poof—it's gone. You can't remember one thing?"

"Yeah," Julie said. That had happened to her lots of times and she didn't think anything of it.

"That's terrible to waste dreams like that. You got to harness them. Ever since I was little I been harnessing my dreams. You know what I told you about my turtle?" She snugged up a curler next to Julie's ear. "Ever since then I been paying attention. I can bring those dreams right up out of the id and write them down. That's what I tell my clients to do. Write 'em down. Not everybody knows it but dreams have messages for us. Dreams," she said, looking out the window toward the sun, "dreams are our past and our future. Our heaven and our hell. The teeniest dream can unlock the deepest secret if we pay attention." She looked back at Julie. "Five dollars a minute is cheap."

Julie nodded. She really wanted to ask about when she was born and how much she weighed and what Loretta thought of her. She wasn't all that interested in dreams, but since it was important to Loretta she tried to pay attention.

"I dreamed one night about a motorcycle on fire going down a white mountain into hell."

"My father," Bagley explained. "He was a motorcycle racer."

"And a good-for-nothing bum. A fast-talking, down-in-the-ditch water rat."

Julie sucked in her breath and looked at Bagley, but he only grinned. "She was crazy about my father," he said, hunching his thin shoulders with delight.

"Go fry an egg," Loretta said, shaking up a little, blue plastic bottle she had taken from the perm box. "Where's that cotton?" She put the bottle down and opened one of the big cabinets, rifled around until she found what she was looking for—a long, fat loop of cotton. She wound it expertly around Julie's head, tucking it neatly behind her ears and beneath the curlers at the nape of her neck. She grabbed a towel from the top of the dryer and draped it over her shoulders. "Ready," she announced, tipping Julie's head forward and squirting the warm liquid all over her head. She put the bottle down. "My luck," she said, "I always fall for the deadbeats, the lowlifes. They wring me dry and then check out. Course," she added, "Sidney checked out permanently. Not that he wanted to."

"He crashed his motorcycle," Bagley said. "He was going down this hill and—" He pushed back from the desk to demonstrate. "Like this—yoooowwwww—and at the bottom was this rut—all sand, see, and then over there, this big, big tree. And he hit the sand and just spun around and hit the tree going ninety. Blam!" Bagley smacked the hand that was the motorcycle into the hand that was the tree.

"Stupid gump," Loretta said, pulling Julie's head backward and squirting across her forehead. "Anybody takes a two-year-old on a motorcycle deserves to get killed."

"That's how I got paralyzed," Bagley said, scooping up a handful of curlers and staring at them.

Julie dabbed at her forehead with a towel and looked up at Bagley in amazement. "How can you be so calm? Aren't you at least mad at him?"

Bagley shook his head. "I wish he didn't die. He was stupid maybe but he was my father. And he loved me. Didn't he, Ma?"

"Yeah," she said, "yeah, he loved you. But if I'd paid attention to that dream I never would have let him take that motorcycle out the next day. I just didn't have a clue to what the message was. Or that one about your father either, Jewel, the little scammer."

Julie sat up straighter. "W-what?"

"See, the night I met him, the very night, I had a dream. Come on over to the laundry tub, Jewel. We gotta rinse you down. Kneel on this."

Julie knelt on a chair and hung her head while Loretta squirted her hair with the spray nozzle. She listened to Loretta's voice over the sound of the water.

"Me and Richie—that's his name, Richie, were walking around Graceland—Elvis's place, you know. And we find this baby in a pink blanket right out on Elvis Presley's patio where he takes his massages. And Richie picks up this baby and he goes, 'Hey, look, there's Elvis.'

And I look around but Elvis isn't there and when I turn back, Richie is gone and so is the baby." She squatted down so she could look into Julie's eyes. "It was a premonition, hon, of him dumping me."

Julie lifted her dripping head and looked at Loretta. "He dumped you?" she said in a thin voice.

"He was a heartbreaker from the get go," Loretta said, energetically blotting the curlers with the towel. "I admit I threw myself at him even though I knew he didn't do a blipping thing but suck up his mother's money buying Chesterfields. He was a good-for-nothing dropout. Next man I get is going to be rich. That's a promise, everybody."

Julie's cheeks were burning. Her father was nothing but a high school dropout?

"And I can't say he wasn't sweet," Loretta said. "He wrote me a song. How'd that go now?" She set down the bottle and stepped in front of Julie and Bagley, shaking her hair back. "I'll never eat corned beef hash again," she sang, "I'll cut off my ponytail, I'll give up cigarettes and whiskey, too, if you say you'll be my little gal." She shook her head. "Pppsssss—I said I'd be his gal all right, in the only way I knew how. He just didn't want to be my guy. He took off for Nashville before I even had the chance to tell him I was PG. Just as well," she said, rewinding a curler and snapping it crisply against Julie's neck.

Julie swallowed hard. "He didn't even say good-bye?"

Loretta stopped talking. "Oh, crud on a crutch, look at you." She took Julie's hand and squeezed it. "Jewel, Jewel, Jewel. You never wanted to know that, did you? Diarrhea of the mouth, that's what I got. Oh, I'm sorry, hon. He was just a kid. Richie Perch, that was his entire name. Richie was a nice kid. Not husband material but a sweet guy."

Julie took a deep breath. "No big deal."

"Ma." Bagley pushed up his glasses and frowned.

"Crap on a cracker, Bagley. I know it. I talk too much. Don't you think I know it? Look," she said to Julie, pulling on her own hair. "Don't go into a blue funk about this. Richie Perch is not your father. Just because he performed that one teensy, little act does not make him a father."

Julie shrugged and looked out the window. She felt like someone had kicked her in the stomach.

"A guy that rides a cow past the first-floor windows of every classroom in J. Liggett High School during final exams is not going to be awarded Husband of the Year. Never mind father."

Julie turned around.

Loretta crossed her arms over her chest, seizing several strands of her silver and gold beads between her fingers. "That's nothing. Do you think someone who filled the municipal swimming pool with fish can be trusted?"

"He did that?" Julie asked.

"Perch!" Loretta shrieked. "He put perch in the pool. Of course they caught him. Who else would put perch in the pool? Goldfish maybe."

"What else?" Julie asked, suddenly interested.

Loretta didn't answer right away. "Get me that gray bottle, Bagley. No—the other one. Shake it. Harder. Here." She tipped Julie's head forward and Julie felt the cold liquid on the back of her neck. She snuffed loudly, feeling waterlogged. "What else?" she repeated.

"Oh, nothing. Unless you count all the Elvis sightings. Those were just for a lark—just to see if he could get people to show up. And they did. Come to think of it, that's how I met him. She shook her head. "What a con man."

"He sounds kind of—I don't know—fun," Julie said, smiling.

"Fun!" Loretta shrieked. "Fun? Richie Perch was crazy. He was wild. Yeah," she said, swinging her beads around and around. "He was a barrel of monkeys."

"She was crazy about him, too," Bagley said, giggling.

"Were you?" Julie asked. "Did you love my father?" Just asking the question made her insides shake. "My father." She had never said that to anyone in her life—meaning who she meant when she said it to Loretta.

Loretta snorted. "Well, look. I was seventeen years old. My mother was dead and gone, my father was a drunk. And there was this good-looking guy who was nice to me, who bought me a charm bracelet and drove me around in his blue Mustang and even wrote a song for me. Yeah, I loved him. You could say that."

Julie closed her eyes. "I can't believe it," she whispered. "I can't believe it."

Loretta put her hands on her hips. "Whatdya mean? What can't you believe? That I loved Richie Perch?"

Julie kept her eyes closed because the tears were right there, ready to spill out. She shook her head. "You can tell me these things. Everything I've ever wanted to know, you can tell me. What did I look like?"

"Huh?"

"When I was born? What did I look like?" She was trembling all over.

"Aw, let's see. You were scrawny, really scrawny. And your eyes were stuck shut so I couldn't see the color. But I thought you were a princess."

She couldn't stop shaking. She had lived without knowing for fourteen years. And now she could know it all. Loretta, her beautiful, wise, courageous mother could finally tell her who she was. But when Loretta unrolled the curlers and Julie stared back at herself in the laundry room mirror, she didn't have any more questions. The person staring back at her with April mist gray eyes and cascades of curly yellow hair was Loretta's daughter, Jewel Young.

8

"Your hair," Mrs. Solus said, after she returned that Sunday night. She dropped her overnight bag and sank to the sofa. "What did you do to your hair?"

"Oh this?" Julie patted her hair in what she hoped was an offhand manner. "I got a perm. My hair was so boring it looked like—" She considered it for a moment, then seized Loretta's expression— "like a prairie dog."

"You had a permanent without even consulting me? Oh, Wayne, look—just look what she's done with her hair. She's ruined it."

Mr. Solus had barely noticed Julie's hair when he got home from the office Saturday night. "You look sprightly"—was what he said. And they sat right down to eat the smothered quail Mrs. Solus had fixed ahead of time because smothered quail was what they had every Saturday night. Julie and her father were comfortable with each other. Julie ate in silence while her father held teeth X rays up to the chandelier and studied them under the light. "Cherry pop," he would mutter or, "Candy bars." He set down the X rays and stabbed his quail with a vengeance. "Next his mother is going to ask me why he needs eight fillings. Boy, that really gets my goat."

Julie thought about Bagley Wonder and his perfect little teeth.

"Does coffee make cavities?" she asked, reaching over for her father's coffee cup.

He shook his head. "Jitters—not cavities."

Julie took a big gulp of coffee while her father sprinkled pepper over his quail. It burned the back of her throat but she was starting to like the hot, bitter taste. She wondered if Bagley would get as jittery as Loretta if he kept drinking coffee. But if it made him jittery Loretta wouldn't let him drink it. She might not be as fanatical as Julie's mother about Bagley's diet, Julie thought, but she wouldn't let him drink something if it was bad for him.

After dinner Julie cleared the table while her father went off to soak his feet in the bathroom. When she got out to the living room he was sitting there with his pant legs still rolled up to his knees, reading his dental journals. Every once in a while, he would lean over and pat his bare feet with a big, fluffy towel.

Once, Julie had asked her father if he had all the money in the world and a chauffeur to take him wherever he wanted to go, where he would choose to go. He thought for exactly three seconds and said, "To the bathroom to soak my feet." She didn't think it was one bit funny. If she ever reached the age of fifty-six and couldn't think of something more exciting to do than soak her feet, she would rather be a cow standing out in the rain all day. In fact, she would rather *be* the rain. Something that didn't have feelings, that couldn't play or dream or listen to music. Her father, she thought, was just about as exciting as a gray drizzle.

"Okay if I practice?" Julie asked.

He glanced up and waved his hand. "Play—"

"I'm going to play 'Starfisher,'" she announced before he could say, "Meet me in St. Louie, Louie."

She pushed back the fall board and started to sing. "Casting in the night with a pocketful of sun, fishing for a star till I caught a little one . . ." She was singing for Bagley, imagining the words winging through the air all the way to Potatoville where he sat missing her. Her heart was suddenly so full she felt if she held any more happiness she would rise off the bench and fly up to the moon. Every day she woke up thinking of Loretta sitting under her rainbow and Bagley at his desk gluing together his kites and when she was going to see them again. Every night before she went to sleep she pulled the covers over her head and said good night to them, right out loud. They belonged to her just as much as her parents did.

And somewhere in the world, she thought, was the man named Richie Perch, who wrote beautiful songs and made people laugh and, who maybe didn't know it, but was her true father. "Richie Perch," she said out loud, imagining what it would be like to have Richie come find her, too. He would see that Loretta was still crazy about him and they would fall back in love and get married all because of her. "Richie Perch," she said again.

"What's that?" her father said, looking up.

She whirled around on the bench to face him. "If I ever have a son, I'm going to name him Richie."

"Good," he said. "I'd like a rich grandson."

"I'm not kidding," she said. "I'm going to name him Richie Perch." She looked at her father for his reaction.

He frowned. "Perch? You're going to name my grandson after a fish?"

"Yes," she said, starting to giggle, "and he's going to be wild. He's going to drive around in a red convertible with the top down even in the winter and he's going to sing at the top of his lungs." She turned back to the piano and started pounding the keys. "I'm from Borneo-eeo-eeo, I drink rat's blood eeoo-eeo, and crunch their bones—eeo—eeo, I sleep on thorns in—"

"Stop." Her father threw up his hands. "I surrender. You can name him Napoleon Bonaparte if you will never play that song again."

"How about this one then?" Julie hadn't planned on playing her song about Loretta. The music just oozed up from her heart, through her fingers and out her mouth. It was all too wonderful to keep inside her. She closed her eyes and started to sing in her torchiest voice:

Homeless and orphaned and thrown out on her own
The beautiful maiden was heavy with child,
Tortured and hungry and oh, so alone
She gave birth to her baby way out in the wild.

Julie opened her eyes and looked at her father. He had started reading his magazine again. She hit the keyboard with all ten fingers. "Dad!"

"Whatsat?" He looked up startled.

"Who is my mother? Who is she?"

"What are you talking about?"

"Describe her."

"Well, she's a lovely, middle-aged lady, slightly portly with a—"

"Dad!" She glowered at him.

"Oh, very well." He scratched the top of his head. "She has pink cotton candy hair and a pink dress and silver wings. And big, shiny teeth," he added.

"You are not one bit funny—in case you think you are."

Sighing, he put down his magazine. "She was a young woman, Julie. A girl, really, who had no options. Pregnant, unmarried, poor. Smart enough to know she couldn't take care of you."

"But what did she look like?" Julie insisted.

"Ah, me." He scratched his head. "I imagine she looked like you. Blond, sprightly, good teeth. To your mother and me she'll always be the good fairy."

"Listen, Dad, you know that song I was playing?" Julie felt giddy again.

He nodded thoughtfully.

"Did you like it? I mean, did it—did it seem special to you in any way?"

"Why, sure," he said. "I like all Frank Slater's stuff. Say, how about 'There's No Remedy.' "

Julie turned around and slammed down the fall board. Betrayed. She had been ready to open up her heart, to tell him her very deepest secret and he hadn't even been listening.

And now, with her mom back home, she felt betrayed again. Her father looked at her hair and said, "I really did like it better the other way, Julie."

Julie leaped up from the love seat. "You never even noticed my hair. I could have dyed it green for all you care. You don't notice anything. You're just siding with Mom, as usual."

Lying in bed, Julie looked over at Jacquelina in the window seat. She sat all day and all night looking out of her blue painted eyes in whatever direction Julie pointed her, her head full of air, no confusion in her heart. Julie envied her. Julie wanted to go to her parents and throw her arms around them and tell them she loved them and that she would wear her hair anyway they liked and that she was lucky to have a mother and father who took such good care of her. But *Jewel*. *Jewel* wanted to run away. *Jewel* wanted to sit in Loretta's kitchen and drink coffee and turn on the oven and light matches and answer the Dreamlines. *Jewel* wanted to sing "Starfisher" at the top of her lungs with Loretta and Bagley singing along. *Jewel* wanted to live in Dreamland.

When she fell asleep, Julie dreamed that she was standing alone in a dark, frozen potato field, holding a green shopping bag, when out of nowhere came a single, searching light. As the light grew bigger and brighter, Julie saw that it was the eye of a huge, black locomotive, whistling over the snow directly at her. Just as it was bearing down on her, it changed into a gigantic, panting dog. When it leaped, Julie grabbed it by its ear and jumped on its back. The dog ran faster and faster, streaking over the countryside, leaping houses and lakes. Julie was breathless, her wild, curly hair billowing out around her face. Soon, they started leaping entire states. Indiana, Nebraska, Colorado, Utah. They jumped over the Grand Canyon and Julie let go of her bag. All her grandmother's plates went falling into the Grand Canyon. Below her, she could see the plates spinning against the night like white galaxies. And then, she lost her grip on the dog's ear. She fell like a rag doll, down, down, down, into the deep, dark canyon.

Julie sat up in bed, her heart pounding. She shuddered, hugging herself. Switching on her lamp, she pawed through the books on her nightstand, looking for the list Mrs. Og had given her. LORETTA'S DREAM LIST, it said at the top. "Apples," she read, "Arrow, avalanche." She went to the D's. "Dog—a symbol of friendship, happy times in good company. But a dog that attacks means you have an untrustworthy friend."

Was the dog attacking or was it being friendly? she wondered. Loretta had told her to write her dreams down, so she found a pencil and wrote it all out in the back of Loretta's dream book. Maybe she would ask Loretta about her dream, she thought. She was the expert. Julie switched off the light and went back to sleep.

When Julie came to the breakfast table, her mother was there, reading the milk carton. She looked up. "Where did you get that beret?"

"Megan," she said, spooning sugar into her oatmeal.

Then her mother saw the pin. "I thought you didn't like that brooch."

Julie shrugged. "Maybe I do now."

"Well," her mother said appraisingly, "I wouldn't have chosen to pin it on a hat. It's a lapel pin. Or here." She demonstrated, holding an imaginary pin at her throat. "You just don't look like yourself, Julie. That whole effect is rather, mmm," she stirred the air with her hands, "rather beatnik looking." She sighed. "Well, at least that wild hairdo is covered up."

Julie nodded. She had hoped her mother would forget about her hair entirely. "How's Grandma?"

Her mother stood up to dump a vase of droopy white lilies in the basket under the sink. She shook her head as she rinsed out the vase. "Jell-O," she said. "That's what they give her for lunch in that place. Red Jell-O and toast. It's a mercy I thought to bring the broiled chicken. Although she's having trouble chewing these days. Maybe meat loaf," she mused. "Who did your permanent?" she asked abruptly. "Annette?"

Julie caught her breath. "It was, uh, a new girl. In fact, it wasn't even at the Hair House. It was the place where Megan and Holly go. They had to get haircuts so I figured—" She shrugged and took off her beret. "You're right about this pin. It looks freaky." She unpinned it and held it out, hoping to distract her mother.

"And how did you pay for it?"

Julie hated how her mom played detective, asking a million questions about the smallest, most insignificant things. "I've got money. You know, my birthday money."

Her mother went to the counter for her purse and pulled out a fifty-dollar bill. She laid it on the table. "You know we pay for your haircuts, Julie. Your birthday money is for treats—to go to concerts or shopping with your girlfriends."

"But, Mom, I don't want you to pay for it. You don't even like my hair."

Her mother handed her the money. "I just hope you consult with me next time."

Julie felt like a criminal taking the money but what could she do? It made her feel guilty but it also made her angry. As if by paying for the perm, her mother was letting Julie know she was still the boss. It was like having the last word.

At least at school her hair was a hit.

"Marlene Dietrich," Mr. Annelin said, stopping at her desk and bowing. As he passed out the list of U. S. senators, he said to the class, "We have Marlene Dietrich in our midst."

"Yeah," she said, pretending she knew who he was talking about. "I'm signing autographs after class."

When Megan saw Julie, she pulled off her beret and screeched. "I absolutely love your hair. Who did it?"

She took a deep breath and clutched Megan by the arm. "Listen to me, Megan. My mother permed my hair."

"Your mother? " She started laughing. "Give me a break."

Just then Charlie lumbered up and dropped his arm over Megan's shoulder. "Nice 'do," he said, pointing at Julie's hair.

"Come on, who did it, really? Annette?" Megan asked.

Julie looked at Megan and Charlie entwined together. She couldn't tell them. She couldn't even tell Megan. She had another life. Julie had another life. That was all. "Right," she said and walked away, thinking that there wasn't another soul in the world who understood her. Except for Loretta Young.

9

Julie got off the bus and looked over at the café. Ike was washing the windows inside and rapped on the glass when Julie waved. She noticed a new sign over the door: IKE'S GOOD FOOD in red letters. So he's been fixing the place up, she thought. Maybe she would go in and eat there sometime. She could take Loretta and Bagley some afternoon if Mrs. Og and Cramp would manage the phones.

She walked down the sidewalk, realizing this was the first time she had been to Potatoville when there wasn't a foot of snow on the ground. It was the middle of March and the muddy ground had become a catchall for winter's litter. Pressed into the brown earth along the sidewalk were old newspapers, pink and yellow handbills, a child's striped mitten, and a Christmas wreath, complete with a smashed red bow. In Loretta's yard, flocks of gray birds were picking red berries off the muddy lawn.

When Loretta opened the door she took one look at Julie and put her hand over her mouth. "Ohmigod, what did you do, rob a bank?" She pointed at Julie's beret.

Julie put her hand to her head and felt the brooch. "Oh, that," she said. "It's ugly, isn't it? I don't even know why I wore it."

"Ugly?" Loretta shrieked. "It musta cost a fortune. It's to die for."

"Honest?" Julie's heart leaped up any time Loretta gave her a compliment. She had never had the nerve to wear the brooch out of the house before, not even to Springhill, where the residents fussed over anything new. Sometimes though, when she took the pin out of Jacquelina's hair and looked at it, the glittering red stones struck her as glamorous instead of gaudy. Then the pin looked like a jewel she might wear to an exotic ball or a half-lit, underground bistro. It looked like a thing of enchantment, like a wishing stone. It was something then, for her other life, her life with Loretta. Now that she knew Loretta liked the brooch, she knew that she did, too. It was glamorous and exotic, full of mystery. It suited Jewel Young, she thought, dropping her jacket on the chair and smiling at Mrs. Og, who was on the phone.

The click of toenails against the floor alerted her that Winston was coming. She grabbed a dog biscuit from her bag and chucked it at his feet as he came into the living room. Winston stopped long enough to drool on Julie's shoe before he snatched it up. "Nice doggie," she said, ducking behind Loretta.

"Bagley's downstairs," Loretta said, picking up the bag from Wong Lee's. "Cramp's got him doing twenty chin-ups. God, I'm such a feeb, I can't even do one. Hey—I got a couple of palms to read back there"—she pointed down the hall—"in the circus room. You wanna answer the phones with Mrs. Og? Just come back and get me."

Julie hesitated. Her own dream had prompted her to read through Loretta's dream book, but she still didn't understand any of the stuff about the buried subconscious.

"Don't get nervous," Loretta said, putting her hands on Julie's shoulders. "Here's the trick—you don't have to *be* a pro, you just have to sound like one. Just read the card, smooth as butter, see, and then come and get me. Say, 'Excuse me, but I need to research just one small item.' They love thinking their dream is so unusual that it's got you stumped. It's simple." She pointed a purple nail. "I'll be down in the circus room—you know, the orange room?" Without waiting for Julie's answer, she hurried away, her bracelets jangling.

Julie picked up the phone and called her mom to report in. As soon as she put the phone down, it rang. Julie snapped her rubber band and looked at it. Mrs. Og was on the other phone, talking about rhubarb with someone. "It can be very sveet, it can be very sour. Like love." She nodded sympathetically. Then she put her hand over the receiver. "Can you get dat, Sveetface?"

Julie took a deep breath and picked up the receiver. "Hello?" she said. "I mean, the Queen of Dreamland. Do you have a dream you'd like to share?"

"I have a dream all right," the man said. "I dream I'm having a baby. And I'm not even married. I'll bet you never heard that one before, did you?"

"Hmm," Julie said. "Before we examine your dream, there are a few things you should know." She read him the information about the buried subconscious.

"So what are you saying?" the man asked. "Are you saying I'm repressed?" He sounded angry.

"Repressed?" Julie repeated. She remembered Loretta's advice. "Oh, no," she said, "certainly not. I believe you are a very extremely unrepressed person."

"That's not what my ex says," he growled. "She's the one that made me call you."

"Hmm," Julie said. "Maybe *she* should be calling Dreamland."

The guy snorted. "Yeah," he said. "You think my dream is weird. Let me tell you what she dreams."

Julie looked at the clock. The man had already been on for three minutes and they hadn't even gotten to his baby dream yet. "Well, fine," she said, trying to sound as soothing as Mrs. Og. "Why don't you do that?"

He talked for another two minutes before she excused herself to get Loretta. "I just need to research that one part about the hatching. I'll be right back, sir."

"You're a doll," Loretta said, when they were back in the kitchen heating up the Chinese food. "That guy was a forty-dollar bill."

"Forty dollars!" Julie looked up from the carton of subgum she was opening. "I didn't even tell him anything."

Loretta laughed. "He didn't want to hear anything. He just wanted to talk. The poor guy was lonely. I coulda kept him on for another ten minutes but I didn't have the heart."

Julie sat at the kitchen table while Bagley and Loretta got lunch ready. From his wheelchair, Bagley got out two pans from the bottom cupboard. He dumped rice in one and Marshmallow Fluff in the other. Loretta handed him a frying pan for the sweet-and-sour chicken; he set all three pans on the stove and turned on the burners. Loretta's movements were just like Bagley's, quick and sure, as she poured the coffee, opened the silverware drawer, and clapped a lid on the rice. As she took down the plates Julie caught her breath. They were the same chipped, dingy plates she had used before. "What happened to the plates—my grandma's plates?"

"Sammy The Pawner." Loretta ripped off three paper towels and tossed them on the table. When Julie didn't respond she looked up. "I pawned them for twelve dollars."

"You—you mean—"

"That's right," Loretta said sharply. "We need the cash more than we need hoity-toity plates. See?"

Julie nodded, speechless. She knew people sold cars and boats and motorcycles to get money. But plates? Her grandmother had

had those plates for fifty years. "I don't care about the plates," she said finally. "I just didn't know you needed the money so much."

"You wouldn't understand about things like this," Loretta said.

"I'm not a little kid—" Julie protested.

Loretta laughed. "No—you're a rich kid. You're different than we are, Jewel. You probably eat toast off those plates and don't think a thing about it. With us, it's scrimp and scrounge, pinch and save. And there's never enough."

"What do you mean?" Julie said. "You said you weren't starving. And you have clothes. And furniture and stuff."

Loretta yanked at her hair. "Look, Jewel," she said, "it's not for those kinds of things I need the money. Bagley and me—what do we need—a can of soup, macaroni and cheese. It's for—"

"For my operation," Bagley said. "So I can walk again. There's this doctor who can fix me, maybe. Guess how much he wants?" Bagley threw back his head and laughed. "Only seventeen thousand dollars." He grinned and scooped out a spoonful of Marshmallow Fluff from the pan and ate it.

"Wise guy." Loretta raised her hand pretending to smack him. But she lifted his baseball cap and kissed the top of his head. "My little wise guy, Bagley Wagley."

"Oh." Julie nodded. She had never imagined Bagley walking. "Gosh," she said to Bagley, "that would be great. I bet you really miss walking and running around and stuff."

He laughed. "I don't even remember when I could walk. I was too little."

"But how come you have to wait? I mean, can't you just get the money from your father or somebody?"

Loretta snorted. "My father? Jewel, I don't know where my father is and even if I did, he wouldn't have an extra seventeen dollars, let alone seventeen thousand."

"Really?" Julie said. "He's broke? My grandfather?" It gave her a thrill to say it, to remind Loretta that she was part of Loretta's family, too.

"Yep," Loretta said. "Your's and Bagley's grandfather. The bum."

"Well, how about our other relatives," Julie offered. "Hasn't anyone got money in our family?"

"Only you," Loretta said, shoving her hair back. "But you're on the wrong side." She laughed. "No, you're on the right side. Rich people can get pins put in their joints, have their gall bladders chopped out, gold crowns put on their teeth and it doesn't cost them a cent. Look at Bagley—he didn't do a blipping thing to cause this accident, neither did I, but we gotta pay through the nose because we're broke. We got no insurance. Doesn't that scorch you?"

"But that's not fair!" Julie said. "If you have to wait until you raise seventeen thousand dollars Bagley could be old. He could be my age. We have to do something right now."

"Sure," Loretta said. "We'll stick up a bank. Want some?"

Julie shook her head and watched distractedly while Loretta dumped Marshmallow Fluff on her and Bagley's rice. "That stuff will rot his teeth," she said to Loretta.

"Bagley, as soon as you finish, you'd better get your toothbrush. First, eat some of this." She spooned some sweet-and-sour chicken on his plate. "Protein," she announced, when he made a face. Julie wanted to make Bagley strong and healthy.

She wanted Loretta's and Bagley's lives to be a hundred percent perfect now that she was here; she wanted them to wonder how they ever existed without her. She pictured Bagley running across a field of daisies, on legs healed by the surgeon that she was able to hire, Loretta saying tearfully, "If it weren't for you coming into our lives, Jewel, honey, we would have been ruined." Money, she thought, money would fix everything.

"Hey!"

Loretta and Bagley looked up from their food.

Julie rummaged in her Harrod's bag for her wallet. She took out the fifty that she had planned on depositing in her bank account. She handed it to Loretta. "This belongs to you."

"Really?" Loretta took it and put it in her blouse pocket. "What's it for?"

"My mom thought I got my perm at the beauty shop. So she paid for it."

"She like it?" Loretta pointed at Julie's hair.

"She hated it."

Loretta and Bagley and Julie all started laughing as if it was the funniest joke in the world. Suddenly, Julie was glad her mother hated her hair. She wasn't the least bit like her mother. She was like Loretta. She was like Bagley. The three of them were joined in blood.

"Listen, you guys—" Julie jumped up from the table and faced them. "I'm going to be a singer, sing in nightclubs, go on tour, stuff like that, and make lots of money. And all of it, every penny," she emphasized, "is going to go for Bagley's operation."

"Wow!" Bagley clapped his hands.

"Aw, Jewel, wouldn't that be a kick? You, a world-famous singer."

"Listen," Julie insisted. "I just wrote my best song. Want to hear it?"

"Well, naturally we want to hear it, don't we, Bagley? When it's on all the charts, we can say we heard it first."

Julie pulled a chair over to the kitchen doorway and stood on it. She looked down at Loretta with her bright golden ringlets, both arms jingling with bracelets as she pulled a chair up in front of the table and pulled Bagley over next to her.

Julie held up an invisible mike. "Ladies and gentlemen, I would like to dedicate this song to my" —she swallowed— "my mother,

Loretta Young." It was the truest thing she had ever said and she wished she really was on stage so she could tell it to the whole world. Tears stung her eyes when she started singing:

Homeless and orphaned and thrown out on her own,
The beautiful maiden was heavy with child.
Tortured and hungry and oh, so alone
She gave birth to her baby way out in the wild.

Julie took off her beret and clutched it to her heart, looking right into Loretta's eyes.

Poverty forced her to give away her jewel,
She wandered in heartache all over the land,
For over ten years she felt just like a fool,
Until her lost jewel before her did stand.

Lost baby, lost baby, before her did stand.
Lost jewel, lost jewel, again in her hand.

She jumped off the chair and bowed.

"Yeah!" Bagley said. He whistled through his teeth.

"Did you like it?" Julie looked at Loretta.

Loretta was silent, her face as pale as milk. Then she reached over and crumpled a paper towel to her eyes.

Julie stared. She had never seen Loretta cry. "Loretta?"

Loretta buried her face in the paper towel and shook her head. "Go on, Jewel—you just made me sound so good, so brave. Like I'm Joan of Arc or somebody."

"But you *were* brave, you *were* noble," Julie said.

Loretta waved her words away like mosquitoes.

"No, really," Julie insisted. "I see everything differently now. I understand why you gave me away. How could you keep me when your own father threw you into the cruel world?"

Loretta blew her nose. "I should have, Jewel. If only I had kept you. If only I had. That was the biggest mistake of my life."

When Loretta said those words, it was as if she had picked up the missing piece to Julie's heart and put it into place. For the first time in her life Julie felt whole.

10

Julie, I am extremely upset."

Julie got up from the dining-room table and took the cordless phone into the kitchen. "What's wrong, Mom?" Julie sounded guilty. She knew she sounded guilty because she knew what was coming. Megan had called her before dinner to warn her.

"I called you at Megan's this afternoon simply because Grandma was having a bad day and I wanted her to hear your voice and Megan said you were in the bathroom and I called again later and she said you were washing your hair and I called yet a third time and—"

"I know, Mom." Julie took a deep breath. "Megan was trying to cover for me. It's not her fault. I didn't go to her house today like I said. I'm sorry."

There was a silence. Then, "I'm waiting, Julie."

"See, Mom, I know this is going to sound weird and you're probably not going to believe it but I went to Springhill to visit one of the old people—Mr. Chesterton. He broke his leg last week and he doesn't have any family to visit him and the bus was going right by Springhill, so I just got out on the spur of the moment. I was only going to stay a few minutes but he was so happy to see me and he wanted to play

Fish and, and then he asked what smelled so good in my bag so I opened it and we ate the Chinese food and he was so happy, Mom. I just couldn't leave him." Julie took another deep breath. "I just lost track of time."

Another silence. "You expect me to believe this?"

Julie was prepared. As soon as she had concocted her story she called Mrs. Cook, the director of Springhill, to ask if she had left her sweater there when she visited Mr. Chesterton. "Why, Julie," Mrs. Cook had said, her voice full of cheery surprise, "how sweet of you. I didn't even see you come through. I'll ask Mr. Chesterton, though it's doubtful he'll remember you were even here. You know how foggy he is, especially since he broke his leg."

Now she said to her mother, "I don't expect you to believe me. Call Mrs. Cook. She knows I was there. Just call her. Her number is nine-six-four—"

"Well, really," her mother huffed. "I'm not about to do that, Julie."

"Honest, Mom, I want you to call her. Nine-six-four, two-six-one-eight—that's her number. Call her right now. She gets off at seven-thirty."

She could hear her mother's long, defeated sigh. "Julie, I'm glad you're so thoughtful. I'm sure it meant a lot to Mr. Chesterton. But how do you think I felt, trying to get in touch with you again and again, worrying where you were, wondering if you had lied to me."

Julie apologized three more times, promised to visit Grandma Snoudy soon, and then it was okay. She knew her mother not only believed her, but, in the end, thought she was a saint for visiting Mr. Chesterton. After she hung up, Julie cleared the dining-room table, then went upstairs to her room.

She sat in the window seat next to Jacquelina. She could smell April through the open window—fresh mown grass, the air sweet with blossoms. In another month, her father would take the cover off the pool and her parents would have the neighbors over for their annual pool party. Julie looked down on the blue-covered rectangle, the wide, white swath of cement surrounding it, and the rows and rows of purple-and-white petunias her mother had labored over every day for the last week.

Julie thought about how meaningless it was. Men and women with every hair in place, in fancy, expensive clothes, standing around the pool eating fancy, expensive food, having a bartender mix fancy drinks with orange slices and maraschino cherries in them. And nobody swimming. Nobody even looking at the pool. The whole thing was a big waste, she thought. Feeding all those people who already ate and drank too much when her parents could feed all the hungry people in town. They could pay the doctor bills of all the children who needed surgery in Oakland County.

Thinking about her parents depressed Julie. Right now, her mother was at her grandmother's house, probably broiling a lamb chop for her dinner. Julie was certain that her mother was thinking about what a thoughtful daughter she was. She could picture her telling Grandma Snoudy the next day about Julie stopping to visit a lonely old man in a nursing home. She hated it that her mother thought she was wonderful, hated it that she believed all the lies Julie had been telling her for over three months. When her mother cooked Julie's oatmeal in the morning or asked her whether she wanted celery or carrots in her lunch bag, or took Julie out in the yard to show her the new shoots on her Alister Stella Gray rosebush, she was talking to the Julie she had known for fourteen years. She hadn't a clue that Julie's whole life had been turned upside down, that Julie didn't care one bit about rosebushes or carrot sticks.

What she cared about was Loretta, her mother, and Bagley, her brother. But there was no way to tell her mother the truth. They just drifted farther and farther apart. She put her chin in her hands and looked at the darkening sky. The Big Dipper looked like it might tip over and begin pouring starlight into the swimming pool. But it was millions and millions of miles away. That's how far apart Julie was from her mother.

Julie must have screamed because she woke with her arms around Jacquelina and her father bending over her, concerned. "Are you all right, Julie?"

She shook her head, trying to clear away the images. "It—oh, Dad, it was a huge dog— a big, black dog." Already the dream was fading. Her father settled beside her in the window seat and she let her head rest against his chest, breathing in the comforting, soapy smell of his skin.

He put his arm around her. "Are you sure it wasn't the Ar Ar come back to haunt you?"

She smiled at him. When she was six, her father had taken her to a county fair where there was an exhibit with a two-headed bear. She and her father named it the Ar Ar because it growled out of both heads. The Ar Ar used to give her bad dreams but that was years ago. She shook her head and hugged him. "I'm okay, Dad. I can't even remember what woke me up anymore."

But after her father left, pieces of her dream started to come back. She got out the blue book and started writing it down. It was just like the other dream but worse. If only she could ask Loretta, but they always ran out of time. She looked at her clock. It was only eleven. She knew Loretta stayed up until midnight. That's when she cleaned house. She wondered if it would be all right to call her. Even though she had her own line, the result of a hard-fought battle for some privacy, she was a little afraid to call Loretta. She imagined Loretta's bright twangy voice spilling out of the phone and ringing through all the rooms and hallways of her house. She knew it was silly. It's not as if anyone could even hear them talking.

She got up and looked down the hall. Her father's bedroom door was closed and his light was off. Julie shut her door and crawled under her covers, suddenly wanting to hear Loretta's voice more than anything. She switched on the lamp and put her glasses on to find the book with Loretta's number.

Beside her, the phone rang. Julie snatched up the receiver before it could ring again. "Hello," she whispered.

"Jewel?"

Julie thought she was going to faint. "Loretta?" she hissed. "Loretta, I can't believe it's you. Is it really you?"

"No," Loretta said. "It's Dolly Parton."

"Ohmigod, it's a miracle. I was just—like right this very instant—going to call you. Honest to God, I was reaching for the phone."

"Yeah," Loretta said. "I figured. I was crawling around on the bathroom floor with a toothbrush trying to get the mold out of the grout when I got this really vibrating image of you. You might's well have been standing on the commode looking down at me for as strong as I felt you in that room. So I called."

Julie felt goose bumps rise all over her body. "Loretta—you're like out of the twilight zone."

"It's not so amazing, hon. It happens with Bagley and me all the time. Your heart calls to me; I don't care if it's at the bottom of a well—I hear you, Jewel. We're connected forever." She snapped her gum. "So, what's up?"

Julie whooshed out a big breath. "Loretta, I have this dream about Winston. I mean, I think it's Winston. And even though I'm hardly scared of him anymore, the dream is scary, really scary."

Loretta's voice got businesslike. "Tell me about it. All the details. Did you write it down?"

"Yeah." Julie picked up the blue dream book and started to read. "It's night and I'm walking down the sidewalk minding my own business when all of a sudden there's this huge train, this big black locomotive coming right at me with its whistle blowing like, 'get out of the way.' Just as it gets to me it turns into Winston and he's going to pounce on me so I grab his ear and jump on."

"That's good," Loretta said encouragingly.

"Then he's like Superman. He zooms up through the sky faster than a comet and I can see my town below me and stars whizzing by and the moon and other planets. But I don't feel powerful, I feel cold and afraid and all alone. There's no one else around—just me and Winston."

Loretta clucked sympathetically.

"It gets worse. He goes so fast I fall off his back into outer space and I've got this bag full of plates—my grandma's plates—and they fall, too, all around me. These hundreds of plates go crashing to the earth. I can hear them smashing below me and then I'm smashing, too, against the cold ground with all these broken plates. And the next thing I know I can't move. I'm in this wheelchair in a glass room and I can see people but they can't see me. I'm calling to my mom and dad on the other side of the glass but they don't hear me. They just go on talking to each other. And next to them are Loretta and Bagley, making a kite. I scream and holler but they don't hear me either. Nobody hears me." Julie stopped reading. "And then I wake up." She sighed wearily, listening to Loretta making popping sounds with her gum.

"It's pretty clear," Loretta said decisively. "Winston stands for change because your life is changing like crazy right now and you're afraid you can't keep up. That's why you fell off his back. And the reason you ended up in a wheelchair? Guilt. Pure and simple. You feel guilty because you haven't told your parents about me, don't you?"

"Yeah."

"So you're caught between them, and me and Bagley, but not with either one really."

Julie nodded. "That's right."

"That'll be twenty dollars." Loretta hooted.

Julie sighed. "So now I know what my dream means, what am I supposed to do about it?"

"Want some advice?"

"Of course I want some advice. Why do you think I almost called you?"

"Don't do anything."

"Yeah, but—"

"If you told your parents, what would they do?"

"Forbid me to see you anymore."

"It would just be opening a can of worms."

"But I have to keep telling these whoppers. Like today my mom found out I wasn't at Megan's so I had to call Megan and give her the Dreamland phone number and tell her I was studying dreams every Saturday. On top of that I had to make up a story about visiting an old man at Springhill."

"She buy it?"

"Yeah, but one of these days I'm going to get caught. I just know it."

"Cross that bridge when you come to it."

"I want to tell her," Julie insisted, thumping the mattress with her fist. "I want to tell her I've found my real mother and she's pretty and smart and she doesn't look anything like a pink fairy with silver wings. And she doesn't try to hide things from me. What nationality are you?"

"Huh? Oh, Dutch on my mother's side and Hungarian on my father's."

"See," Julie said. "Nobody ever told me before. "I'm Dutch-Hungarian. I'll bet they knew that all along. And what nationality is Richie Perch?"

"Gee, he never told me. Let's see. I'll betcha he was Italian. He had that black hair like Italians, you know? And he really liked pepperoni pizza."

"Well, whatever," Julie said. "The point is you tell me what I want to know."

"Listen, Jewel, they probably want to pretend it didn't happen, that I never existed. That they're the ones who gave birth to you. It's their corpuscles, or whatever, running around inside you."

"That's the stupidest thing I ever heard of."

"People like to fool themselves," Loretta said. "Listen, I gotta get back to work here or I'll be scrubbing the toilet at four in the A.M."

"I'm glad you called me," Julie said wistfully. "Do you think about me when I'm not there?"

"Every breathing second," Loretta said. "Honeybun," she added. "I borrowed that word from Mrs. Og."

"Well," Julie said, not wanting to hang up. Then she thought of something. "You know those plates in my dream? I've got dozens of them down in the basement and I want you to have them. You can pawn them to raise money for Bagley's operation."

"Aw, you're a peach. But are you going to keep bringing them in that green bag? It'll take you a year."

Julie hadn't thought of that.

"Tell you what." She snapped her gum two or three times. "I'll come over in Cramp's truck this weekend. We'll load 'er up."

"What!" Julie yelled so loudly she clapped her hand over her mouth. "You can't do that," she hissed.

"Well, you said your mom and dad are both gone on Saturdays. Nobody home. We get rid of the plates that you don't want anyway. And make a wad of money. Where's the problem?"

Julie gulped. "What if someone sees you?"

"You got a garage? We'll park the truck in the garage."

What could happen? Julie thought. Her parents would be gone. The nearest neighbor was half a block away. It was crazy, thinking about bringing Loretta into her house. Her mother would kill her if she found out. But her mother would be almost two hundred miles away, Julie thought. What was the big deal? It would be wild to have Loretta and Bagley in her very own house, to bring them for the first time into her world. Wild.

11

It was a blustery spring day, with a wind that sent garbage can lids spinning down Washington Street. Rain blew in sheets in front of the bus when Julie got off. Lifting the Harrod's bag over her head she raced for her house, not seeing the blue truck until it pulled away from the curb and started honking.

"Jewel, Jewel. It's us!"

Peering through her wet glasses, Julie saw Bagley leaning out of the truck window in his shirtsleeves, waving wildly. It was so peculiar to see Loretta and Bagley in her neighborhood that Julie stopped on the sidewalk and stared at them. Then she glanced quickly in both directions to see if any of the neighbors were looking. "This way," she yelled, motioning for them to follow her. As Loretta drove the rusty old pickup toward the garage, Julie made a dash for the back door to click open the garage door. "Hurry," she yelled through the pelting rain.

After she and Loretta lifted Bagley and his wheelchair through the doorway and into the laundry room, Julie took off her raincoat and looked at them. "You guys are soaking," she said, handing Loretta a folded towel from the top of the dryer. "And where's your jacket?" she asked Bagley. "You're not supposed to go out in this weather without a jacket." She handed him a towel and took another to wipe down his wheelchair.

"We don't have a garage as big as an airplane hangar," Loretta said. "In fact, we got no garage at all. Me and Cramp had to fool around out in the rain, loading him and the wheelchair and naturally the wheelchair gets all wet back there in the truck bed." After she mopped at her face, Loretta fluffed up her hair with both hands and tossed the towel into the wicker hamper. She whistled. "Wow." She called back from down the hall, "get a load of that piano."

"Hang on," Julie said. "Wait for me." She wanted to run down the hall and bring Loretta back. Her stomach was jumping up and down. She felt the same way she did when she and Megan snuck into the school once on a Saturday morning to break into Charlie's locker and see if he had a picture of Eva Voorheis taped inside. Julie wasn't even supposed to be here after her piano lesson. What if someone looked in the window and saw Loretta walking around in the living room? But then she relaxed a little, remembering that her mother always closed the drapes before she left the house.

"Hey—you look like you went through a car wash," she said, looking down at Bagley. She took off his glasses, wiped them on her shirt, and put them back on his nose. His hair was plastered down like it was painted on, and his teeth were chattering. "Geeze, Bagley—" She squatted down beside him. "Why didn't Loretta make you wear a jacket?"

"She was too excited," Bagley said, hugging himself.

Julie pushed Bagley's wheelchair down the hallway to the living room and parked him next to Loretta, who was playing "Chopsticks" at the piano. "I'll be right back." She ran upstairs and quickly called her mom at the nursing home. Then she yanked two sweatshirts out of her drawer and a crocheted afghan from the foot of her bed.

Loretta kept on playing "Chopsticks" while Julie pulled Bagley's wet T-shirt off, pulled on a big red CANOPY CHARGERS sweatshirt, rolled up the sleeves, then tucked the afghan around his thin little body. She offered the other sweatshirt to Loretta.

Loretta shook her head. She plucked her damp, red and white polka dot blouse away from her and fanned it in the air. "This is grandiose," she said, lifting her feet and twirling around to the other side of the piano bench. "I been dying to know what it would feel like to grow up in such a grandiose house with a grandiose piano and tons of pretty things—" She spread her arms to take in all the vases and statues and wall paintings in the room. "And a swimming pool." She stood up. "Where's the pool? Hey, too bad we didn't bring our suits."

"Ma—it's raining," Bagley said, pulling the blanket up to his chin. "You never go swimming in the rain."

Loretta put her hands on her hips. "Izat so? Well, when I was a kid, I—"

"Listen," Julie said, snapping her rubber band. "Maybe we should just get started here. Get the stuff from the basement and clear out."

"Oh." Loretta turned to Julie. "Look at yourself," she said. "Your face has all gone to chalk. All week long Bagley and me have been planning this like it was an outing to the Waldorf Historia. Talking about Jewel's grand piano, Jewel's beautiful big bedroom. Jewel's this, Jewel's that. Chandeliers dripping like diamonds all over Jewel's big, old gorgeous house." Loretta's cheeks turned bright red as she went on. "And you hate us being here, don't you? We're making you have an agitation attack."

"Don't get mad," Julie said quickly. "I love you being here—you and Bagley. I'm just a teeny bit nervous, that's all. Like what if my father walks in? Or what if the Avon lady comes to the door? Or what if Cramp's truck gets a flat tire in the garage and we have to call a tow truck?"

Loretta rolled her eyes.

Julie giggled nervously. Loretta was right, she decided. She was overreacting. "Okay," she said, taking the handles of Bagley's wheelchair. "I'll give you a tour of the whole house."

Loretta picked up every candlestick, every china bird, every candy dish. In the kitchen, she dropped onto one of the green topped stools at the center island, moving her head in quick, birdlike motions to take everything in. "This is enormous," she breathed. "You could make dinner for the whole of the Detroit Pistons in here. And their wives." She tapped a lilac fingernail against the green counter. "Cordivel, isn't it?" she said to Julie.

Julie shrugged.

"Costs twelve dollars a foot," she said to Bagley. "It's what I think is in the White House kitchen. Only blue. And lookit the refrigerator. It matches the floor. Bleached oak floor, bleached oak door. You had that made special, didn't you?"

"I don't know," Julie said. She had never really noticed that the door and the floor matched. She couldn't believe Loretta was so impressed by the refrigerator. "Wait," she said. "I'll show you something else." She got a glass out of the cupboard and held it against the metal bar. Half a dozen icy stars clinked into the glass. "Here." She offered the glass to Bagley.

"Star-shaped ice cubes." Loretta slapped her cheek.

Bagley peered into the glass like it was full of diamonds. He looked up at Julie, wide-eyed behind his glasses. "Could I do it?"

Julie hugged him. "You can make a million ice cubes." She got another glass out of the cupboard and handed it to him. "Just press it against that metal bar."

The ice maker rumbled and ice started clinking into Bagley's glass. He held it there until it was full.

Julie turned to give Loretta a knowing smile, the kind of smile she and her mom exchanged when a little kid at the mall would break away from his mother to come over and show them his brand new sneakers. But Loretta had disappeared.

"Look," she called from the dining room. "Look at this, Bagley." She waltzed back in with a ruby-colored vase of roses. "Red roses in a red vase." She held the roses under Bagley's chin and he sniffed and nodded. Then he rolled his wheelchair over to the sink and dumped the ice. He rolled back and started filling the glass again.

"It's not even for a special occasion, is it?" Loretta asked, burying her nose in the center of the blossoms.

"My mom just loves roses," Julie said. "They're no big deal. She grows them all over the yard and gives them weird names. That one's Rio Samba, I think."

"Oh, Rio, Rio Samba," Loretta crooned, dancing around the kitchen with the vase and making clacking noises with her high heels on the wood floor. "One time back in Tennessee I got roses. On my thirteenth birthday. A deliveryman brought them to the door. 'These flowers are for Frances McDonald,' he goes. 'Right here,' I go, holding out my arms."

"You didn't," Julie shrieked. "You took somebody else's flowers?"

"I loved them way more than she would have. I kept those roses until they turned black. Besides, it was my thirteenth birthday. It was meant to be."

Julie stopped laughing. "Didn't your dad ever bring you flowers? Like when you lost your first tooth or when you did something great like pass your polliwog swim class?"

"Polliwog swim class. Ha!" Loretta set the vase down and opened one of the bleached oak cupboards. "Look at all these glasses. Not a jelly jar in the bunch. Nope. I coulda drowned in my polliwog swim class if I ever had one and my old man wouldn't have brought me roses." She took out a goblet, pinged it with her fingernail, and set it back on the shelf. "Hey, can I see your upstairs?"

While Bagley played with the ice maker, Julie took Loretta up to see her bedroom, her parents' bedroom, the guest bedroom, and the bathrooms. Loretta exclaimed loudly when she saw Julie's canopied bed, kicking off her shoes and climbing up on the mattress to closely examine the beribboned flounce that hung from the posters. She fingered the gold faucets in the bathroom, even the Oriental rug in the hallway, like museum pieces. The more impressed Loretta was, the more self-conscious Julie became. When Loretta finally suggested going to the basement to bring up the dishes, Julie was relieved.

"Yoo hoo, Bagley. Do you want to come down with us?" Loretta called. "Me and Jewel together can carry you."

"Jewel—can I stay here? Can I keep making stars?"

Julie came to the kitchen doorway and grinned at Bagley. He was almost lost in the giant red sweatshirt and his hair stuck up every which way. "What are you going to do with all those ice cubes?" she asked, pointing at the sink.

"I'm going to take them home—can I?" he asked breathlessly. "I'm going to put them in my pop and stuff. Maybe, hey, maybe I can take them in my thermos to my teacher."

Bagley was so excited over the ice cubes that Julie wished she could give him the whole refrigerator. "You're a pretty cute brother, Bagley," she said, kissing the top of his damp head. She got a plastic dishpan from a cupboard and set it at his feet so he could fill it with ice cubes. "We'll be downstairs," she said, "if you need anything."

Unlike most basements, this one was filled with beautiful furniture, antiques that Mrs. Solus had collected or inherited—velvet love seats and padded benches and a gleaming walnut dining-room set. In one corner, between two Windsor chairs was a lovely old cherry chest. It had been a hope chest for several generations of women in Julie's family. When it had belonged to Julie's mother, she had filled it with her Aunt Julianna's flowered dishes and with fancy sheets and nightgowns Julie's grandma bought her long before she was old enough to marry. Now it was full of finery meant for Julie when she became a bride. But, at fourteen, Julie had no interest in domestic things and believed she never would. She was happy to contribute it to Bagley's cause.

"Holy cow!" Loretta said, taking the lid off one of the boxes. "Ritzy stuff." She lifted out a silver sugar and creamer that Julie had often seen on Grandma Snoudy's breakfast table and held it up to the light.

"Why don't we just leave everything boxed up?" Julie suggested. "That way, we can carry it upstairs easier."

"Aw, Jewel. I just want to look at this stuff. Boy oh boy, if my mother had only had just one piece of this, just this little precious creamer, for instance, I betcha she would have stuck around."

Julie blinked. "What? I thought your mother was dead."

Loretta shrugged. "She might as well be. Wow." She jumped up and went over to where the clothes bar was. "Look at this big old mink. Your mom's?"

Julie nodded. "But why did you tell me—Loretta."

"I just want to try it on. Don't have a hairball." Loretta slid into the dark, shimmering mink and twirled around. The coat was so huge on her it would have swept the floor if she weren't wearing high heels. She held out her arms in a pose. "How do I look?"

"Stupid," Julie said hotly. She was annoyed that Loretta had lied to her about her mother. And it upset her that Loretta was more interested in her grandmother's dishes and her mother's mink than she was in talking to Julie. Loretta put on her mother's coat like she was in a department store where she could take anything off the rack and try it on.

"Oh, c'mon, Jewel, this is fun. Get in the party mood." Loretta shoved up the sleeves of the mink and started going through the hope chest. "Oh, my God. Look at all these Hummels in here." She held up a little Dutch boy carrying water pails. "You know how much these things go for? There's a fortune, just in Hummels, in this chest." She took out another Hummel—a little ballet dancer in a pink tutu—and examined it. "Hey. Instead of pawning this stuff we could advertise in the paper. Have collectors come to a big sale. Like a garage sale. Only no junk."

Julie sank down in her father's old black leather chair and looked up at the narrow glass windows that ran along the basement ceiling. The light coming in was yellow, but it was still raining. She could hear the steady plop of raindrops and the drip of water from the downspouts. She snapped her rubber band in time to the sound, wishing she had never agreed to this. She thought of her mother coming down here and opening the hope chest. She pictured the look of horror on her mother's round, wrinkled face, the way she put one hand on top of the other over her heart. What if she called the police, Julie thought. Could Julie be arrested for stealing her own things?

"Hey." Loretta came and stood over her, flapping the sleeves of the mink in her face. "What's eating you, Jewel? What are you being so moody for?"

Julie glared up at her. "All you care about is money."

"What?" Loretta put her hands on her hips. "This isn't for me, all this stuff. We're going to sell it for Bagley's operation. But there's no law I can't enjoy looking at it for a minute, is there? Just because you've been mollycoddled your whole entire life, had everything brought to you on a silver platter—"

"I have not been mollycoddled." Julie snapped at Loretta. "You're the one making such a big deal out of this—oohing and aahing over every little candlestick, prancing around in my mother's mink coat."

"Your mother?" Loretta put her hands on her hips. "Your mother? Let's just get something straight here. It was *your mother* who landed you in this big, fancy house with gold faucets. If *your mother* hadn't put you where all the money is, you'd be wearing clothes from Ernie's Basement instead of The Country Lady, and you'd be eating macaroni and cheese for dinner. You should get down on your knees every night to thank *your mother* for finding you this gravy train to ride all the rest of your days."

Julie stared at her. "What are you talking about? Like you searched all over the country until you found my rich dad and my rich mom to take care of me? That is such a big crock, Loretta. Besides, it doesn't matter to me one single bit if there are gold faucets in the bathroom. I already told you that. And I could eat macaroni and cheese every day of my life."

Loretta snorted. "You say that because you got a choice. Rich people always have a choice. They say, 'oh, money's not everything. I could live the simple life easy. Go off and live in a cabin somewhere. Fish and hunt.' Ha."

"I hate that," Julie said, breathing harder. "When you talk to me like I'm from another planet just because we have more money. It's like you—" She paused to think about it. "You're jealous, that's what. You want all this stuff for yourself. You criticize me when I didn't even ask to have a fancy house, but you would snap it all up in one second. You're jealous, aren't you?"

"Now listen," Loretta said, red circles standing out on her cheeks, "you think you know so much about life but you don't. So just shut up and I'll tell you. It's no picnic to worry about your little boy all the time because he can't run around and kick cans and climb trees. Because he's got no friends. Because he sits inside and makes kites all day long and turns white. You never sat up at night and worried about what if I don't get the money together for his operation? And what if he has to wheel around in that chair till he's an old gray man, always wearing spotless tennis shoes because his feet have never touched the ground? And aluminum foil. How do you think it feels to keep washing out aluminum foil to use over and over again and to wear Salvation Army underwear?"

Loretta ran her hands over the mink coat. "My mom always warned me to not be like her. She never had one nice thing in her life, not even a little old rabbit jacket." She picked up a crystal bud vase and traced the pattern with her fingernail. After a moment she murmured, "There were only those flowers she almost got. From my dad."

Julie had been sitting motionless, barely breathing. She couldn't believe that she and Loretta were yelling at each other. Her heart was pounding in her chest so hard she could hear it in her ears. But, finally, Loretta's words sunk in. Those few, stumbling words that came after the sharp torrent of anger. In that moment, she understood why Loretta loved the gold faucets in the bathroom. And she understood why she was so angry. "The flowers?" she asked carefully. "From the deliveryman?"

Loretta nodded. "Frances McDonald. She left us forever on my thirteenth birthday. Only two hours before those roses came."

"Oh," Julie said, putting her hand to her mouth. "Oh, Loretta."

12

Julie's mother wanted her to visit Grandma Snoudy the second weekend in May but that was when Loretta was having her yard sale.

"Next week," Julie said, looking around for her piano books. "Next week, for sure. Mrs. Wigmore just got in the sheet music for me to play at Mrs. Gully's birthday party Monday night. It's one of those ancient songs she loves— 'Stardust,' or 'Deep Purple' —one of those. You'd think, once in a while, one of those eighty-year-olds would want to hear some Van Morrison or even Elvis, but no—it's gotta be something from the Dark Ages." Julie was talking too much, hoping her mother would go out the door. "Gee, Mom, it looks like a great day for your drive. The sun is shining, not a cloud—"

"Julie, your grandmother is one of those eighty-year-olds," Mrs. Solus said firmly. "She would love to hear you play, too."

"Oh, I know, Mom. Next week I promise. I'll practice 'Surrey with the Fringe on Top,' just for her. Promise." She gave her mother a big smile. "Geeze, I forgot my beret. I've got to run back upstairs. Tell Grandma I'll see her next week."

Julie hummed all the way from her piano lesson to Loretta's. She didn't even realize it until the old man sitting next to her said, "My, it certainly is nice to hear someone singing like a bright, little chickadee. Of course, if I was a pretty young thing with my whole life ahead of me, you can bet I'd be singing, too."

She smiled at him when she got up and he tapped the brim of his crumpled hat. Walking down Penny Lane, toward Loretta's, Julie felt like she wanted to open her arms and hug everything. Three little boys were sitting on a front porch in their pajamas eating graham crackers and smacking their bare feet against the sidewalk. The quick slapping sound mingled with the other sounds in the neighborhood, a barking dog, somebody hammering in one of the garages. All the little houses with their scraggly yards and squashed bushes were full of kids and dogs and fathers who stayed home on Saturdays and fixed things in the garage and mothers who hung clothes on the line. Julie could see one now, pinning up a big, pink sheet and talking to a baby in a jumper seat. She couldn't believe she had once been afraid of this neighborhood. Now, it was as if she had lived here her whole life. She had family here, she thought, waving to Bagley as she came up the walk.

"Wow," she said, looking over the tables of sale items, things spread out on the lawn, on newspapers, and old army blankets. There were even clothes hanging from tree branches with little yellow stickers on them. "Where did she get all this stuff?"

"We begged from the neighbors," Bagley said cheerfully. "We told them it was a fund-raiser for my operation and they gave us tons of stuff. Look."

Next to the house was a rustbucket of a car. The sign said, RUNS GOOD—$300.

"Geeze," Julie said. "Where's the dishes and stuff from my house?"

"Up on the porch." Bagley pointed.

On one side of the porch sat Cramp looking miserable, his big body hunched over a tableload of china and crystal. The sign over his head said, THE GOOD STUFF, with an arrow pointing down.

Loretta was sitting on the other side of the porch dressed like a fortune-teller in a long, black skirt with red braid around the bottom and a red shawl that had once draped the dining-room table. She had wound a bright red turban around her head and secured it with a round plastic pin that said, IKE'S GOOD FOOD. She was reading someone's palm when she spotted Julie, but she jumped up and waved both her arms in the air. "Jewel, hon—I'm up here. Let me borrow your pin, okay?"

Julie unpinned the brooch from her beret and handed it up to Loretta. "I never saw so much stuff in my life," Julie said, looking around the yard.

"Can you believe it?" Loretta adjusted her turban and handed the IKE'S GOOD FOOD pin to Julie. "People started knocking on the door at seven-thirty this morning. And not just lookers, either. We sold three Hummels at fifteen apiece and a couple of the good vases and there's this lady coming back with her husband for a whole dinnerware set that I said she could have for eighty dollars. Hey—Cramp—did you see that lady yet?"

He shook his head morosely, his earring flashing in the sun.

Loretta giggled. "Looks ready for hanging, doesn't he? He can't stand all these people around him."

Behind her, the person sitting on the stool said something. "Oops," Loretta said. "I'm doing a reading, Jewel. I made a place for you over at that aluminum table. There's a pink box of change. We take checks, no charge cards. Everything's priced in nice round numbers on the bottom. Mrs. Og is inside minding the phones and baking pies. If you have any questions, ask her." Loretta flounced back down into her chair, snatched up the waiting woman's hand, and began studying it.

Julie sat down in a folding chair next to a plastic jewelry box with

Miss Piggy on the top. She lifted the lid; inside were compartments for nickels, dimes, and quarters. She was surprised at how organized Loretta was, collecting all this rummage, pricing it and arranging it on tables so professionally. If there was a trick to everything, as Loretta said, then she seemed to know all the tricks. Maybe being poor made you smarter, Julie thought. Like Abraham Lincoln.

She looked across the yard at Bagley who was sitting at a table full of pies. His sign said, MRS. OG'S FAMOUS BERRY PIES—ONLY $5. Beside Bagley was a canister with a photo of him in a wheelchair. It said, CONTRIBUTIONS TO THE BAGLEY WONDER FUND GO HERE. A man who had just bought a pie dropped some change in the jar and patted Bagley on the head. The sunlight poured down on his hair, making it look like there was a bright halo over his head. He was laying down dollar bills in a shoe box one at a time. As soon as he straightened them, he picked them up and started counting them all over again.

Here she was, for the first time in her life, Julie thought, doing something important, helping someone she really loved. Loretta was right. She had been pampered, living in a fancy house, wearing expensive clothes, taking piano lessons, getting a fat allowance for doing nothing. She thought about Loretta getting excited over those roses on her thirteenth birthday. The day her mother left her. Julie's heart ached just thinking about the sadness Loretta had lived with. She was here for them now, both of them. Whatever it took, she would make them happy. Just thinking about it made her smile.

She grinned up at her first customer, a man who paid her three dollars for a silver toaster with a handle missing. She sold a brass vase for four dollars, and a Mr. and Mrs. Potato Head salt and pepper shaker set for two fifty. And a whole bagful of clothes for eleven dollars.

"Hey, good lookin'. What's so funny?" Ike crossed the lawn with a tray of food. He was wearing a chef's hat with three IKE'S GOOD FOOD buttons pinned to it.

"Hi, Ike," Julie said. "I'm just having a good time, that's all."

"Here—this'll keep you smiling." He handed her a plastic-wrapped bun. "Ike's famous potatoburger," he said. "Grand opening special." He felt in the pocket of his apron and handed her another Ike's button. "Mind pinning this on?"

Julie pinned the two Ike's buttons she had to her beret where the brooch had been. She sat back and watched people's reactions when Ike handed them a potatoburger. It was like being in the grocery store when they passed out chocolate chip cookies. Even if folks were scowling when Ike came up to them, they cheered right up when he gave them a free sandwich. People were the same no matter if they were poor or rich, she thought, unwrapping her potatoburger. It tasted like warm, spicy french fries, with a hint of mustard and onions. Better than a Coney Island. "Umm," she said, looking across the lawn at Ike and giving him the thumbs-up sign.

"Aaaah, excuse me, miss, but could you interpret—do you think aaah, a dream. I understand the charge is, aaah, ten dollars."

Julie looked up to see a thin man in a blue suit. He was holding out a ten-dollar bill. "Oh, you want Loretta," Julie said, pointing up at the porch.

"Aaah—" He pinched his nose like he was about to go under water. "Aaah, she is occupied and you—" He pointed at a sign on the table that Julie hadn't noticed before: QUEEN JEWEL INTERPRETS DREAMS—$10.

"Oh," Julie said. She put down her potatoburger. "Well." She couldn't believe Loretta hadn't told her she'd be interpreting dreams. She would have brought along her dream book at least. "I'm not that good," she said, shaking her head. "Not as good as Loretta. Wouldn't you like to wait for her?"

The man shook his head and placed the ten-dollar bill next to Julie's potatoburger. He sat in a folding chair across from her and leaned forward, his watery blue eyes bulging over his striped tie. He licked his pale lips. "This is the dream of, aaah, of a friend of mine."

If he hadn't been so nervous, Julie could never have talked to him. "Okay," she said, taking a deep breath. She told him everything she could remember about the unconscious. Then someone interrupted them to buy a lady bug ashtray, along with a package of unopened pencils and a bun basket. She put the money, along with the ten-dollar bill, in the plastic jewelry box. "Tell me everything," she said, trying to sound like Loretta. "Everything you can remember."

"This friend?" he said questioningly.

Julie nodded at him to continue.

"He, aah, often, has dreams about a woman who is a, aah, aah—"

He looked like he was going to choke. Julie glanced around for a glass of water.

"She floats," he said abruptly, folding his arms over his chest.

"In water?" Julie asked.

"In air," he said, heaving a big sigh.

"Well," she said doubtfully. "It's not much to go on."

He nodded and started to get up. "I understand."

"Wait," Julie said. "Let me think about it a sec." She looked at him sitting there so poker-faced and stiff in his blue suit. She wanted to tell him to at least loosen his tie. Here it was late spring and Saturday and he was dressed like the chairman of General Motors on his way to the office. She rubbed her temples like she had seen Loretta do. "A lot depends on your friend—how he feels about this dream. Does it make him happy dreaming about the floating woman or does it make him sad? Worried? Excited?"

"It makes me—aah, I mean it makes him—" He sighed and hung his head, as though Julie had caught him in a lie.

Julie felt sorry for him. He was so nervous, so unsure of himself. "It's okay," she said. "Whoever."

"Duane!" Loretta came flying across the lawn, clutching her skirt with one hand and her turban with the other. "Duane, I never in a millennium thought you would show up here." Loretta threw her arms around him and kissed him, leaving red lip prints on his white cheek.

"Did you meet Jewel? She's my daughter and over there— Oh, I guess I forgot to tell you about Jewel, didn't I?" Loretta said when she saw the expression on Duane's face. "I'm too young to have such an old daughter, that's what you're thinking, isn't it?" Without giving him a chance to answer, she told Julie, "He invents computers, can you believe it?"

"Well, aah . . ." Duane held up a finger. "That's not precisely correct. Computers have already been invented. I merely—"

"Come on up here, Duane, and I'll read your palm." Loretta took him by the hand and started tugging him in the direction of the porch. "For free. And then you can figure out what you want to buy. We have some boffo things on the porch."

Duane gave Julie a pleading look, and she suddenly realized the floating lady was Loretta. Maybe, she thought, he didn't want Loretta to know he was having floating dreams about her. He was such a nerdy guy, she couldn't imagine Loretta being interested in him. She was probably just buttering him up for a killing in the china and crystal department. She watched Loretta lead him up the steps to the porch. In a way, she was sorry she hadn't had more time to work on his dream. She picked up her potatoburger and took a big bite, thinking about how she could have won his confidence, gotten him to recall other details. After all, interpreting dreams was in her blood. She was like the junior Queen of Dreamland.

"Little lady, I wonder if you'd take less than twenty for this bike, here?" A fat, breathless lady was holding onto a red-faced little boy. "I already spent fifty bucks up there, buying a wedding gift for my son and his gal. I only have thirteen left and he" —she jerked her head toward the boy— "wants the bike with the horn."

"Wait a sec," Julie said. "I'd better ask my mother." Julie pointed to where Loretta sat studying Duane's skinny white palm. She started in the direction of the porch just as Mrs. Og came out the front door, flapping her apron at Julie.

"Love Bug," she said, taking Julie by the shoulders. "Your friend, Megan, she called, dis minute."

Julie started to break away. "I'd better find out what she wants."

Mrs. Og put her arms around her. "Sveetface, I'm sorry. I tink it is your grandmama. Dat's what I tink it's about."

13

Julie woke to the sound of a distant cuckoo clock—six cuckoos. She felt for her glasses on the nightstand, but her hand dropped into empty space. Then she remembered and opened her eyes. She had been sleeping in this strange, little room for two nights—since she and her father drove up to Griffinville Saturday night. She looked up at the peaked ceiling that sloped down to the walls. When she tried to sit up her head bumped the ceiling. The attic room had been Mabel's, the woman who cared for Grandma Snoudy for years and years before she died and Grandma was moved into a nursing home. Mabel was dead, Julie thought, and so was Grandma Snoudy.

She felt under the bed for her glasses; as soon as she put them on she saw that it was raining. Julie cringed as if she were personally responsible. The last thing her mother had said before they went to bed was, "I hope it doesn't rain for the funeral."

They had been sitting around the dining-room table eating the pineapple upside-down cake that Mrs. Baldwin, her grandma's neighbor, had brought over. Uncle Fess, her mother's brother, was there with Aunt Helen and Aunt Helen's sister, Bertie, who lived with them. They were waiting for her mother's other brother, Uncle Jeff, who was flying in from Wyoming. Uncle Fess was telling stories. Her mother's eyes were red, partly from laughing at her brother's stories, but mostly from crying.

Julie had wanted to cry, too, not because she was sad about Grandma Snoudy, but because she had hurt her mother's feelings. There wasn't one thing Julie could say to change things, to change the fact that she put off going to visit her grandma dozens of times until, now, it was too late. The only thing she could think of to say to her mother last night when she was hoping it wouldn't rain was that Julie was sure it wouldn't. She was certain it would be sunny for her grandmother's funeral.

But it was pouring. What a terrible day it was going to be, Julie thought, heading for the shower.

Downstairs, Aunt Helen and Bertie were sitting at the kitchen table in their robes, drinking coffee. When Julie came into the room, Aunt Helen stood up to give her a hug. Julie hugged her back, lifting her head so that Aunt Helen's hairpins wouldn't stab her in the chin. For such a small person, Aunt Helen had a very big voice.

"Poor Julie," she boomed, patting Julie's back. "I'm the one who should have slept in that teeny, little room." She pushed Julie down into a chair and looked at Bertie, who was as thin and stretched out as a piece of spaghetti. "Can you believe she made poor Mabel live in that cramped room for twenty years? Why, Mabel was as tall as you are." She pointed at Bertie. "But that was my mother-in-law for you. She believed in the caste system."

She poured a cup of coffee and set it in front of Julie. Then she slapped her cheek. "Oh, lordie, you're only fourteen, aren't you? You'd better have some milk."

Julie shook her head. She sipped her coffee and listened in silence as Aunt Helen went on about her grandmother.

"How your mother put up with her all these years, I'll never know," she said to Julie. "Especially at the end. That woman never said thank you. You could put yourself through the wringer thirty-eight different ways for her and she thought it was her due. How did she cope—driving here every weekend to wait on that old shrew?"

Julie was startled. She put her coffee cup down and looked at Aunt Helen. "My mother didn't think Grandma was an old shrew. She loved her."

Aunt Helen smiled indulgently as if Julie didn't know what she was talking about.

"She loved her," Julie said again. "Every Friday night she spent hours fixing my grandma's favorite foods to take with her. Little biscuits and fruit salads with cut-up pineapple in it and these soft little cookies that Grandma liked in the shape of stars."

"Imagine!" Helen looked at Bertie and rolled her eyes. "What a waste."

Julie felt a rush of anger. It was as if her aunt was accusing her mother of stupidity. "It wasn't a waste," she said hotly. "My mother likes making people feel special." Then, confused by her emotions, she looked away, to hide the quick tears that stung her eyes.

"There, there," Aunt Helen said, patting her arm. "I didn't mean to upset you. I know you miss your Grandma Snoudy."

Julie sniffed loudly and angrily swiped at her tears. Aunt Helen had no idea how Julie felt. It was her mother Julie was crying about, not her grandmother. All those months Julie's mom had been worrying about her mother, trying to make her last days cheerful and comfortable, Julie had been focused on herself. Some Friday nights Julie would come into the kitchen in her pajamas and her mother would still be at the counter, frosting little star-shaped cookies with pink icing. She would give one to Julie. "Is it soft enough? You don't think it's too lemony?" her mother would ask anxiously. Julie had no patience for her concern, no sympathy for her mother's sadness. She only wanted to avoid her mother, to perfect the web of lies that took her away to Potatoville, away from the constant fussing and clucking.

Julie sighed. She had succeeded too well. She picked up the napkin and blew her nose. She hadn't thought once about what it would feel like to have your mother dying and not be able to do anything but bring her cookies.

Julie stood up. "I'm going to take some coffee up to Mom and Dad."

"There's a good girl," Aunt Helen said, as Julie left the kitchen with two cups of coffee, two orange juices, and some slices of pineapple upside-down cake.

Julie was afraid they might still be sleeping, but the bedroom door was open. Her mother was sitting in the rocker, still wearing her net cap and looking out the window. "Room service," Julie said, stepping into the room.

Her mother's face brightened. "You brought me breakfast?"

"For you and Dad." Julie set the tray down on top of the dresser.

"Dad's gone to Traverse City to pick up Uncle Jeff. His flight was delayed until this morning." Her mother fluttered her hands at the tray. "But, Julie, you don't have to do this, darling. Breakfast in bed. You're going to spoil me."

Julie handed her mother a cup of coffee. Since her father wasn't there, she took the other cup for herself and sat on the bed facing her mother. "Sorry it's raining, Mom."

Her mother shook her head. "No matter, really. It's just that she always—" She looked into her cup and sighed.

"What?" Julie sat forward, suddenly curious about this woman who was her grandmother, her mother's mother. When her mother didn't respond, Julie went on. "I wish I had known her better. I should have. I'm—I'm sorry, Mom, that I didn't go with you all those times."

Her mother sipped at her coffee, leaned back in her chair, and looked at Julie. "I'm sorry, too, dear."

"I can only remember her in bed or lying on the sofa listening to me play the piano." She had a vision of Grandma Snoudy, as large and unmoving as a snow sculpture, propped up on the sofa in a white nightgown. Her eyes though, were like bright, blue stones. Julie could feel them watching her as she played.

Her mother tipped her head to one side and started to sing in her quivery voice, "Chicks and ducks and geese better scurry . . ."

Julie started to sing along. ". . . when I take you out in the surrey, when I take you out in the surrey with the fringe on top . . ." She laughed softly. "Grandma's favorite song. She used to shout the words to me from the sofa. 'Watch that fringe and see how it flutters!' Honest, sometimes she drove me crazy, Mom." She sighed. "Now I only wish I could hear her yelling the words from the sofa. If only I could play it for her one more time."

Her mother dabbed at her eyes with her sleeve and nodded.

"Oh, Mom. I'm really sorry." She got up and put a piece of cake on a plate and handed it to her mother. "Eat."

"Thanks, darling, but I'm not hungry. I just—" She took a tissue out of her robe and blew her nose. "I know she was eighty years old and that she was sick and crabby but I can't believe she's gone." She shook her head.

"You loved her a lot, didn't you?" Julie said. She took her mother's cap off and began unwinding the toilet paper around her head.

"She was amazing," her mom said. "The most amazing woman I ever knew."

Julie lobbed the toilet paper into the wastebasket. "Aunt Helen said she was kind of—of . . ." She groped around for a nicer word than shrew.

"Oh, Helen." Her mother waved her hand in the air. "What Helen knew about my mother would fit in a teacup. Here." She stood up and lifted a black-and-white photo off the wall, then patted the bed next to her for Julie to sit. "She was twenty-seven years old in this photo with three children under seven and my father already in his grave."

Julie looked at the stiff, unsmiling young woman standing next to a marble monument that was carved with these words: SNOUDY MONUMENT COMPANY.

"That was my father's business. He had just started it before he died and my mother took it over. She didn't know the first thing about gravestones or running a business. She had this photo taken to advertise her business."

Julie looked at the photo again. In her stiff pose, Grandma Snoudy reminded Julie of a marble monument. The perfect advertisement, she thought. "Is that why you and Uncle Jeff and Uncle Fess aren't in the picture?"

Her mother shook her head. "They took us away from my mother because she didn't have enough money for rent or groceries."

Julie turned to stare at her mother. "I didn't know that. You never told me that."

"I barely remember," her mother murmured, gazing at the picture. "That's why she looks so angry. They took her children away for a whole year."

Julie felt anger rising in her own chest—the same anger that her grandma must have felt. "But how did she get you back?"

"You've heard of people working their fingers to the bone. That's what my mother did. She set up a cot in the little shed that was my father's business office. And that's where she lived. She worked night and day, learning about marbles, traveling by horseback to families who had lost a loved one, making her sales pitch. It's ironic but it was losing her children that made her such a success." She paused. "But it made her a little—I don't know—a little hard. That's what people like Aunt Helen see."

Julie stared at her mother in amazement. What if Grandma Snoudy hadn't made enough money to come back for her? Her mother would have been just like Julie, raised by a different set of parents.

"I can't believe I didn't know that," Julie whispered. She felt dizzy, like she had just stepped off the Tilt-A-Whirl at the fair. She thought of the facts separately and then together. Her grandma had to give up Julie's mother because she didn't have enough money to take care of her. And her other mother, Loretta, had to give up Julie because she didn't have enough money to take care of her. What did it mean? Was it like a curse? But it didn't make sense—what happened to Grandma Snoudy had nothing to do with Julie. They weren't even related, really. Maybe, she thought, it was just a strange coincidence. Besides, she would never give up any of her children. If she knew anything in her life she knew that.

"You were her only grandchild," her mother said, hanging the picture back on the wall. She sat back on the bed and put her arm around Julie, drawing her back against the headboard.

Cushioned by her mother's ample breasts, Julie sat in silence, looking out at the gray sky. She listened to the cars driving by on the wet street and wondered if rain was filling up the hole that had been dug for her grandma's coffin.

"She adored you," her mother went on. "Oh, maybe she didn't gush all over you. But that's because she didn't know how to gush. That piano downstairs? She bought it just for you. So you could play all the Rodgers and Hammerstein that she loved. She wouldn't even let Mabel touch it. Oh, she was stubborn, Julie. You were her granddaughter all right. Stubborn."

There it was again, Julie thought. It wasn't genes, the way she was related to Loretta and Bagley. Grandma Snoudy didn't even choose her the way her parents had. She was just a woman, like her piano teacher or the lady next door, who happened to be in her life. Who happened to be her grandma. So how could she be like her grandma, who she barely knew and wasn't even related to by blood?

Mr. Solus returned with Uncle Jeff just in time for the church service. Julie held the black umbrella with one hand and took her mother's arm with the other, walking her carefully around the puddles up to the big oak double doors. Her father and Uncle Jeff followed the six men wheeling the big, pearly gray steel coffin down the aisle and slipped into the pew next to them. When she saw Uncle Jeff, her mother leaned her head on his shoulder and started crying again. The minister started to talk.

He talked about a woman named Amanda Snoudy who grew up poor and died wealthy. In between, she gave money to charities all across the country, put several of the town's young people through college, and provided monuments for all who couldn't otherwise mark the graves of their loved ones. She was a woman of substance, the pastor said. A woman of character.

After he was done, he introduced her three children. Uncle Fess got up and told a story about how Amanda Snoudy took up a petition when she was seventy-five years old to get rid of all the billboards within the city limits. "And she was just stubborn enough that nobody could say no to her," he said, smiling at the memory.

Uncle Jeff got up and talked about when he was ten his mother caught him and a friend throwing mud at a police car. "She made us go to the station and volunteer to wash all the police cars." He paused. "And they accepted." There was a murmur of laughter in the church before he sat down.

Then Mrs. Solus got up on the altar, smoothed down her black linen dress, and started to talk. "Everyone knows that Amanda Snoudy was tough and stubborn but most people don't know there was another side to her. For twenty-five years, before she became bedridden, every musical production in this county was underwritten by Amanda Snoudy, anonymously. She loved the songs, the fancy costumes, the frivolity. Yet, in all those years, she never attended a single one of those productions. She would send her three children instead, and we never missed a single one because we had to report back to her. Every song, every little detail. And she made us promise not to tell anyone about her gift. She preferred her image as a tough old lady. But she wasn't," Mrs. Solus said, her voice breaking. "She was gentle and fun-loving. I just wanted you to know," she added. And sat down.

Julie held her breath when Pastor Greenhoe introduced her. She didn't really know her grandmother, didn't begin to know her until these last few days. Would what she was going to do make people feel worse? She glanced at her mother when the pastor said, "And this young lady was very special to Amanda Snoudy. Many times she mentioned to me that her greatest delight was listening to Julie play the piano. For that reason, Julie has asked if she could play her grandmother's favorite song one more time."

Her mother looked at her, startled tears springing to her eyes.

She stood up. "Is it okay?" she asked, ready to sit back down again.

"Go ahead." Uncle Fess waved her on.

She sat down at the little white piano on the altar and hit the first chord. "Chicks and ducks and geese better scurry," she sang. "When I take you out in the surrey—" It was a silly song to play for a funeral, she thought. But it was her last best gift to Grandma Snoudy.

14

Julie lay on the rubber raft in the middle of the pool with a straw hat over her face. Now that it was the end of June, she had given up wearing the red beret. Besides, she thought, it looked naked without her brooch.

Megan sat next to her in an inner tube, talking and making little splashing sounds with her hands. "So how was I to know she was going to break the heel on her shoe and show up in the middle of the afternoon when Charlie and I are making out on the sofa? God, I can't believe it. She walks right in, slams the door, and starts screaming like an air raid siren. 'I trusted you all these months, I trusted you and all this time you've been carrying on like a little sneak. Your father and I were so proud of you, thinking you were taking such good care of your little sister and she could be out playing in traffic for all you care.' And then she starts in on Charlie. 'No respect for our daughter, taking advantage of our hospitality, never darken our door again, blah, blah, blah.' God, Julie, I thought he was going to cry."

Julie had been listening to Megan's ranting for an hour. She lifted her hat and looked at her. "So are you going to slash your wrists?"

Megan flung her head back against the tube and closed her eyes. "No," she said. "You're not going to believe this but in a way I'm glad it happened. At first it was fun having Charlie over there playing house and sending Holly on errands like she was our kid. But I was on the verge of a heart attack all the time. Whenever my mom asked me anything about Charlie I was sure Holly would spill the beans. And, as my mom says, we implicated her, too. Made her lie for us. The notorious Ward sisters brought to justice at last."

"So did your mom forbid you to see Charlie anymore?"

Megan shook her head. "But I've kind of lost interest in him. I'm through with men. They're more trouble than they're worth."

"Oh, right. I'll check with you in another month." Julie turned over on her stomach and handed the straw hat to Megan. "Here. You're going to get wrinkles."

"I don't care," Megan said, throwing the hat up on the cement. "I'm going to become a nun."

They floated in silence for a few minutes. Julie concentrated on her belly button where she could feel her pulse beating against the rubber mat. She couldn't work up any sympathy for Megan. She wasn't even that overjoyed to have Megan's friendship back again. It was an unreliable thing. Just like everything else in her life.

"Hey," Megan said, kicking water on Julie with her foot. "Are you still seeing that dream lady?"

Julie ignored the question and slid off the mat to the bottom of the pool.

Six Saturdays passed without Julie seeing Loretta and Bagley. Now that her mother was home every day, she was trapped. And, since she didn't take piano in the summer, she couldn't even duck in to see them for an hour. Day after day, Julie floated on the rubber mat looking at her mother's purple-and-white petunias through her eyelashes. She pretended she was on an island in the South Pacific where she had escaped with Loretta and Bagley after Bagley's operation. She pictured Bagley skinning up palm trees to toss down coconuts for their lunch while, below, she and Loretta, wearing grass skirts, interpreted dreams for the islanders. In the evenings the three of them would sing together at a beach bar. "Oliohanna, wanna, manna, by my little grass hut where the coconuts grow, I dance the hula hula in the sunset—"

"Julie—telephone."

Julie paddled over to the side where her mother was squatting with the cordless phone.

Before she handed it to Julie, she said, "It's for your class ring. The lady wants to know which style you prefer. When there's a choice, Julie, always take the most classic style. You want to avoid the trendy."

Julie heaved herself up on the cement and took the phone under the linden where there was a wrought-iron table and chairs. Her mother walked behind her rubbing her back with lotion. Julie waited until her mother went back through the sliding doors into the house. "Hello?"

A shrill, falsetto voice said, "When there's a choice, Julie, always take the most classic. You want to avoid the trendy." There was a volley of laughter. "Boy, I had to pass a ten-minute security check to get through to you."

"Loretta?" Julie glanced up to make sure her mother had disappeared. "Why did you call me down here?"

"I called you upstairs four times, Jewel. You're never in your room."

"Well, I tried to call you last night and the night before that and the night before that."

"Duane," Loretta said simply.

"Oh."

"You don't like him, do you?"

"I like him," Julie said. "Just fine. But he's not your type. He's—"

"Rich," Loretta said. "Rich is my type. Guess where we had dinner? The Whitney in Detroit. It's where all the toney people go. The waiters all wear these classy black tuxedos. That's the kind of place it is." She snapped her gum cheerfully. "I wore your pin on my red dress—you know that red dress with the fringe. Kinda flashy? You don't mind do you, Jewel? When are you coming over, hon? Me and Bagley miss you. Bagley's got all the money from the garage sale to show you. All five hundred and forty-seven dollars of it."

Julie sighed. "I'm going crazy, Loretta. My mom never leaves my side. She even wants me to go with her to the grocery store."

"Oh, crud," Loretta said. "I read about a lady like that who, after her husband died, she didn't want to be alone. Clinically depressed," she said. "That's what she was."

"I don't know," Julie said. "I sort of feel sorry for her. I mean, she was really close to her mother and she built her whole week around taking care of her like some kind of Florence Nightingale. And now she's hovering over me the same way. I hate it but I still feel sorry for her. I mean, how would you feel losing your mother?" As soon as she said it Julie wanted to bite her tongue. "I-I mean . . ." she stammered.

"Sitting around feeling sorry for yourself is a luxury," Loretta said. "I could never afford it."

Julie hated it when Loretta said things like that. She didn't even know her mother. How could she judge her? Besides, Julie thought, her mother wasn't sitting around feeling sorry for herself. For two weeks she had been going through all of Grandma's papers.

"Why not get away from there if she's driving you so buggy? Come on over here for the rest of the summer if you don't want to be hovered over. Nobody ever accused me of being a hoverer," Loretta added.

"How could I do that?" Julie hissed into the phone. "She doesn't even know you exist. I mean, she knows you exist but not around here. Not in my life."

"Julie, dear." Her mother was at the sliding doors, holding up a plate of sandwiches and motioning to her to come in.

"I gotta go, Loretta. My mom fixed me lunch."

Loretta didn't say anything. She just hung up.

"I have an idea, Julie," her mother said as Julie finished eating her sandwich. "Look." She held up a yellowed three by five card. "This is grandma's own recipe for chocolate crinkles. She created it herself and do you know, dear, she baked twenty-four dozen chocolate crinkles every Christmas and took them to the Whispering Meadows Home. The very home she ended up in." Mrs. Solus's face darkened. "You would think they would have treated her better wouldn't you?" She shook her head. "Of course, that was years ago."

Julie nodded and started to pour herself a glass of milk.

"I thought we'd bake some chocolate crinkles."

Julie put the milk down and looked at her mother's beaming face. "Now? It's eighty-five degrees out and you want to bake cookies?"

"Well, we do have air-conditioning. It's not as if we'll be baking under the hot sun." She put her arm around Julie. "Think of this as Grandma's legacy, something we can do together in her honor. I think it would make her very happy to look down and see us baking her chocolate crinkles together. And just think, someday you'll be baking them with your own little girl."

Julie sighed and said, "All right."

Her mother read out the ingredients while Julie gathered them. "Two sticks of butter. One cup of sugar. Melt two squares of chocolate—oh, I'd better do that. You put the butter and sugar into the bowl. Get me a fork and I'll just blend this together until it's nice and silky."

Mrs. Solus's large body quivered as she mashed at the butter in the bowl. She didn't trust Julie to do anything but the most basic tasks, like unwrapping the chocolate squares and finding the mixing spoons. Everything had to be perfect and the only way to get perfection was by doing it herself. As Julie watched her mother she thought how different Loretta was. Whenever Julie went there, Loretta needed her to do something. She expected Julie to help out the same way Bagley and Mrs. Og and Cramp helped out. She didn't snatch matches from Julie's hand in a panic when there was a burner to be lit.

On the first warm day of spring, Loretta sent Julie up on the roof to help Cramp clean the gutters. "You can climb out on the roof through the tower room," she said casually. "You know that little pointed room? Just throw the stuff down below for Cramp to rake up."

Julie didn't even know what "stuff" Loretta meant. On her way up the stairs, Cramp called after her. "Gloves, Missy." He held up a pair of gray-and-blue-striped gloves. "Wet leaves," he muttered, looking at his feet. Cramp was so shy he never said more than three or four words at a time, but it was enough to convey what Julie was supposed to do when she got up into the tower.

When she walked into the little, round room Julie felt like she was in a bird cage. She turned around and around, looking through all the windows, and thought of the fairy tale about Rapunzel. "Rapunzel, Rapunzel, let down your long hair." She giggled, imagining letting down her hair for Cramp to climb up to the tower on.

It was a wonderful little room, not at all like the prison cell she had imagined when she first saw it. If she lived in this house, Julie thought, she would clean off all the cobwebs and polish the windows and sit up in the tower writing songs all day long. The feeling of being a bird in a cage made her want to sing. She rolled open the window and stuck her head out. "Tweetle, tweetle, tweetle, tweetle," she chirped at the top of her lungs. Down below, Cramp looked up from raking the dead leaves in the flower beds. He smiled.

Julie was less brave when she stepped out on the roof. Gingerly, gingerly, she put one foot down, then the other, still hanging onto the window. She could almost hear her mother's voice shrilling in her ears. "Julie, for heaven's sake, you're going to kill yourself. Come down from there, this instant. Wayne, Wayne, look at her. She's going to fall."

Taking a deep breath she let go of the window casement. She didn't look down. She looked out, out over the freshly tilled fields, the trees beyond just unfurling the first green of the season. She could smell the earth and the freshness of spring and a little sweetness of blossoms. She felt like flapping her wings and taking off. Taking another step, she tested her footing. The shingles were as grippy as rubber cement. She inched her way down to the gutter and sat on the edge of the roof three stories up. Then she plunged into the brown, wet leaves with both hands and watched them fly to the earth like flocks of brown birds. She wished then that her mother could see her.

"This is fun, isn't it?" her mother said, carefully squeezing brown dough out of a tube onto a cookie tray she had greased. "Here, dear." She handed Julie the spoon to lick. "Don't you think so?" she persisted.

Julie shrugged.

"I mean baking cookies together. It's like Christmas in July." She wiped her hands on a wet cloth and dried them before she slid the tray in the oven. "I feel like we've grown a little apart these past months. Of course, I was preoccupied." She sighed. "We have to do more things like this, Julie."

Julie tried to laugh. "You mean I should spend more afternoons watching you bake cookies."

Her mother looked up sharply. "What do you mean? We baked Grandma's cookies together."

"That's right," Julie said. "I unwrapped the butter, measured out the sugar and handed you the eggs. It was a heck of a good time." She was doing what she swore she wouldn't do—making her mother feel bad.

Her mother slowly washed her hands again in silence. "Well, Julie, I thought we were having a good time," she said, turning around. "It's just that there are some things I'm better at than you are."

"How do you know?" Julie asked. "If you never let me try? How do you know I can't crack the eggs in the bowl or stir them up or set the timer? You told me what a great person Grandma Snoudy was. How she took over the monument business when she didn't know one thing about it. And she became this fabulous success. How would she feel looking down on us this afternoon to see that her fourteen-year-old granddaughter can't even make a batch of cookies? Ashamed, that's how she'd feel. And embarrassed." Julie slammed down the spoon. "Sometimes I'd like to pack up and go live somewhere else for the rest of the summer. Somewhere I'm appreciated."

15

If your father doesn't remember to pick up the whitefish, we won't have a thing to eat except the Harvard beets from last night."

"Whitefish?" Julie shifted the shopping bags she had been carrying for the last four blocks. Her hands had red grooves in them from the weight of the *Eat-for-Health* cookbook, three dozen oranges, and a Juicer-Matic. "But it's Wednesday," Julie said.

"I know it's Wednesday. Just a moment, dear." Her mother dropped her bags and sank down on a bench next to Marshbank Park under a big old shade tree. Her face was red from the heat, and the scent of her White Shoulders perfume filled the air around them. "Whew." She reached in the bag, pulled out the cookbook, and began fanning herself. "I don't know why I ever agreed to this, Julie. It would have been far nicer to take a cab."

Julie started to protest.

"You're right, you're right." Her mother held up her hand. "I need the exercise. Whooo." She heaved another sigh. "I'm not getting any younger." Smoothing her hands over the stomach bulge of her pink skirt, she added, "And I'm certainly not getting any thinner. And that's exactly why we're having whitefish for dinner. Your father's cholesterol is two hundred sixty-seven and Dr. Simpson told him, flat out, to give up steaks, pork chops, hamburgers, roasts—all the foods he loves. 'Wayne,' he said, 'unless you're going to give birth in three months, you'd better do something about that stomach.' " She wrinkled her nose in disgust. "Gut is the word he used. 'Do something about that gut.' Honestly, he talks like a football coach. It wouldn't hurt him to tidy up his—aaaaaah!"

An enormous black dog bounded up to the bench and stuck his nose in Julie's lap. Mrs. Solus grabbed hold of Julie and started shrieking. Julie took one look at the big, boxy nose, the slobbering mouth. "Winston!" she yelled. "Oh my gosh, wait, Mom." She peeled her mother's fingers from her shoulder and stood up.

"Julie!" her mother shrilled behind her. "Get away from that dog."

"It's okay," Julie said. "Look. He wouldn't hurt a midge." Winston was standing on his hind feet with his front paws on Julie's shoulders. She scratched behind his ears.

Gasping, her mother climbed up on the bench and began flapping the cookbook in the air. "Shoo," she said. "Shoo—you bad dog. Julie," she hissed. "Stop touching that filthy dog."

Julie looked behind her into Marshbank Park, past the pond where she used to stand with her feet in the mud, watching for turtles. There, just beyond the monkey bars, sitting all alone in his wheelchair was Bagley, flying a kite. She caught her breath, looking around for Loretta. What was Bagley doing here all by himself? He was so far from home he couldn't have wheeled himself here.

Julie took Winston by the collar and pulled him to the sidewalk. His toenails made a scratching noise against the cement as he danced around her, licking her knees.

"Julie," her mother whispered. "Come up here beside me and we won't make a sound. Maybe he'll lose interest and go away."

"You stay there, Mom. I'm going to take this dog back to his owner. That's him over there. I'll be right back." She tugged Winston between the bushes behind the bench and started out toward Bagley.

"Julie, come back here," her mother wailed.

"You can sit down now, Mom," she called over her shoulder. "Just relax." She and Winston ran past the merry-go-round and the red swings to the wide, open grass where Bagley sat in the sunlight, looking up at the sky. There, his King Monarch dipped and rose like a bright orange bird.

"Bagley!" she called.

Bagley turned in his wheelchair. His two little arms shot out for her, knocking the string ball from his lap. Winston happily pounced on it.

For a brief second Julie wondered if her mother was watching, but she flung herself at Bagley anyway, smushing her face against his sweaty, little cheek and knocking both of their glasses askew. She was so happy to see him again that she felt tears stinging her eyes. She pulled back to look at him, adjusting her glasses. "What are you doing here, Bagley?"

He poked up his glasses with his finger and said soberly, "Waiting for you."

"Waiting for me?" Julie sank back on the grass, laughing. "But how did you know that I would walk by? How did you know that I would even see you from the sidewalk? If it hadn't been for Winston, I never would have looked over here. Besides, I never come to this park anymore. Not for years, silly."

Bagley grinned down at Julie. "But you came today."

Julie pulled out a handful of grass and threw it at him. It landed on his baseball cap like green confetti. "What are you, Mr. Wizard or something?" Saying that reminded her of Loretta and she looked around again. She spotted her mother still standing on the bench, peering at them over the shrubbery and waving the cookbook. Julie waved back. "Hey, Bagley, I gotta get going. Where's Loretta?"

Bagley leaned down and pulled the ball of string away from Winston. He looked at Julie and shrugged.

"What do you mean?" Julie said, standing up and looking around in earnest. "You're not all alone, are you?"

"She's coming back to get me," Bagley said, unreeling more string. The kite jumped once and sailed off toward the dark line of trees at the back of the park. "Want a donut?"

Julie put her hands on her hips. "She couldn't have left you all alone, Bagley. All alone in this big park in a strange part of town."

"She didn't," Bagley said cheerfully. He pointed at Winston. "Winston's with me. And we've got lots of donuts and red pop and stuff." He held up a blue thermos beside him on the seat. "I ran out of star ice cubes, Jewel. Could you bring me some more?" He looked at her, his round gray eyes pleading. "Not today, just someday. I miss you, Jewel," he whispered.

Julie looked up into the sky at Bagley's kite. She was trembling. How could Loretta just drop Bagley off at this park? What if it started to rain? What if Bagley's wheelchair tipped over, like it did once when she was chasing him around a tree in his backyard? What if a gang of men came and kidnapped him? What good would Winston be? Julie hated thinking Loretta was irresponsible, especially when it came to Bagley. And why hadn't she packed him a decent lunch instead of red pop and jelly donuts? She shook her head, not wanting to think such thoughts about Loretta.

"Well, it's a terrific surprise," she said, forcing a smile. "I guess Loretta knew how much I wanted to see you, didn't she?"

Bagley brightened and nodded his head.

"Just a minute. I have to check with my mother." She turned to see that her mother had stepped inside the park and was taking a few cautious steps in their direction. She was still waving the cookbook.

"Is that your other mother?" Bagley pointed. "She looks like a grandmother. A nice grandmother," he added.

Julie nodded. "I'll be right back. Hang on to Winston, will you?" She took off back across the park at a fast trot.

"Julie, for heaven's sakes," her mother huffed, when Julie reached her. "What in the world were you doing with that little boy, and why is he sitting there in his wheelchair like a lost sheep?"

Julie licked her lips. "See, Mom, that's just it. He's the little brother of this girl that goes to our school and he's waiting for his mom and I hate to just leave him here all alone."

"Well, really, Julie. That's no concern of yours. If his mother is so neglectful that she left her helpless little son all alone in the park, I think the wisest course would be to call the police."

Julie's cheeks burned at her mother's attack on Loretta. "It's not that she's neglectful," Julie said quickly. "She just went to the store for a few minutes and she left the dog—Winston—to watch him. He's a. . . a trained guard dog."

"He's horrid." Her mother snapped open her purse for a hanky. "Big, black, smelly beast. Come along, Julie. I've got to get home and put my feet up before dinner."

Julie's mouth went dry. She couldn't go home and leave Bagley alone. She was his big sister. If Loretta didn't care and her mother didn't care, Julie did. She had pledged herself to helping him, to taking care of him, to protecting him. She took a deep breath. "Mom—listen." She forced a laugh. "I guess I'm getting to be a worrywart just like you. But I don't feel right leaving him alone. You go on without me—I'll carry all this stuff home." She pointed at the bags. "I know how tired you are."

Her mother was silent for a long moment. Then she said, "Well, perhaps you're right. I would feel responsible if anything befell him.

Though for the life of me I can't imagine why his mother doesn't feel responsible for the frail little thing. I'll come along with you, Julie."

Julie looked at her mother in surprise. "You will?"

Her mother nodded. "But you'll have to tell the little boy to keep his dog away from me."

Julie scooped up the shopping bags and they both started across the park.

"He's so cute, Mom." Julie was suddenly anxious that her mother like Bagley. "His name is Bagley and he's ten years old and he's been in a wheelchair for eight years. And he's as sweet as an angel." She nudged her mother and pointed with her head. "See that kite? He made it. It's called a King Monarch."

"For heaven's sake, Julie, slow down," her mother puffed. "*I'm* not ten years old."

But Julie hurried ahead to set down the bags and grab hold of Winston's collar. "That's my mom," Julie said to Bagley as her mother came huffing past the swing set.

"Hi." Bagley waved.

"Hello, Dagwood," she called back, sinking down on the merry-go-round.

"Bagley," Julie and Bagley said together.

She nodded. "I'm going to keep my distance from your dog if you don't mind. I'm sure he's very nice but I'm a big scaredy cat."

Bagley squinched up his eyes and laughed. "Jewel used to be afraid of him, too."

"Julie," Julie muttered.

"I mean Julie," he said.

"Wherever is your mother, dear?"

Julie glared at her mother. "I told you, Mother. She just went to the store." Julie froze. It hit her that Loretta was going to see her mother when she came back for Bagley. Loretta would know it was Julie's mother but her mom wouldn't know that Loretta was her birth mother. After all these months, her two mothers would meet each other. Her heart started racing. She and her mom would have to leave quickly. That was it. Before they could start chatting.

"Would you like an orange, dear?" her mother asked Bagley. "There are thirty-six of them in that bag next to you." She pointed.

"Oh, no thank you," Bagley said. "I just had two jelly donuts and some red pop. I have lots. You want some?"

The smile on her mother's face faded. "Jelly donuts?" she repeated. "Did your mother pack you a nice sandwich, too?"

"Nope." Bagley laughed and unreeled more kite string. "I just like jelly donuts and so does my mom. Jelly donuts and Marshmallow Fluff. That's good on everything." He looked back at Julie's mom. "Did you ever have that? We have it on everything."

Julie's mother shook her head wordlessly. Then she looked at Julie, her eyes bugging out.

"I bet your mom is real nice," Julie said quickly. "Isn't she?"

Bagley gave Julie a wiseacre look and buried his face in his hands, giggling.

Julie held her breath but Bagley just nodded his head and laughed some more. He was so cute, Julie thought. Couldn't her mother see what a wonderful little boy Bagley was? The world's most perfect little brother, she thought. She could taste the words in her mouth, that's how badly she wanted to say them to her mother. My perfect little brother.

Mrs. Solus continued to fan herself with the cookbook, smiling politely at Bagley from her perch on the merry-go-round. They sat with Bagley for an hour and watched him fly his kite. Her mother kept looking at her watch and sighing, but she didn't complain. "You have nice manners," she told Bagley when he offered to let her fly the kite. She liked him, Julie could tell. Even if she thought Loretta was terrible, at least she liked Bagley.

It wasn't Loretta who came for Bagley. The figure moving across the summer grass looked like a cornstalk in a three-piece suit. He stopped twice to peer at them, as if he might turn and run. But Bagley waved at him and Duane forged ahead.

"We can go now," Julie said to her mother. She jumped up and nodded her head in Duane's direction. "That's his, umm, his—he came for Bagley."

"Well, I must say he looks respectable," her mother said smoothing her hair. "Your father is a nice-looking man," she called to Bagley.

Julie nudged her mother forward. "We've got to run, Bagley. Say hello to Duane for us."

"Well, darling, that's hardly polite. Let's at least say hello to the man."

"Moth-urr," Julie said. "I have to go to the bathroom." She snatched up the bags and bounded off. Duane, she thought as she headed for the sidewalk. Loretta had left Bagley all alone in the park so she could be with that hopeless, tongue-tied sad sack.

16

Julie was sitting in her pajamas at the piano, singing in her most melancholy voice. "Homeless and orphaned and thrown out on her own, the beautiful maiden was heavy with child—" She wasn't trying to sound like Etta Jonas; she was really melancholy. She missed Loretta and Bagley. Their lives were going on without her. She had forgiven Loretta for dumping Bagley in the park. After all, Bagley only wanted to see Julie. Loretta couldn't just drop him on Julie's doorstep like he was a regular friend from school. And Julie couldn't jump on the bus and go visit them anymore, now that her mother was around every weekend. It was a hopeless situation.

Julie kept singing when her mother came into the living room: "Hungry and thirsty and oh so alone, she gave birth to her baby—"

Her mother whisked away the roses on the piano and replaced them with a fresh bouquet. "I thought we'd go in to Pringle's Mall this morning and buy you a new swimsuit. You're bursting out of the top of your blue one."

"—way out in the wild," Julie sang, daring her mother to ask what she was singing. "For over ten years—"

"Julie!"

Julie stopped. "I can't, Mom. I have other plans."

"What other plans?"

She looked at her mother, at the wrinkles around her eyes and mouth. She looked old, broken down. And there was something else, a kind of stiffness in her face. Ever since Grandma Snoudy died, her mother wanted to be with Julie every second, like she was desperate for a friend. It had been over seven weeks since her grandma's funeral and Julie was tired of being buddies with her mother. "Mom, I just don't want to go shopping today."

"Then we'll go tomorrow. If we wait any longer all the swimsuits will be gone."

"But, Mom, I don't want to—" She started over. "Listen, I'm not trying to hurt your feelings or anything, but I don't want to go shopping with you. I mean, I know you've been feeling bad since Grandma died but I need a little more space."

Her mother was silent.

"I wouldn't mind shopping by myself for a change."

"Fine," her mother said briskly. She disappeared and returned with a fifty-dollar bill. "Bring me the change."

Julie went upstairs and got into her shorts and T-shirt. She was going to see Loretta. Julie should have been clicking her heels for joy but she wasn't. She was tired of telling lies, tired of living lies. She was sick and tired of having to sneak upstairs to call Loretta, of pretending Bagley was some little waif in the park.

At the door her mother said, in an injured voice, "Be home by two."

Julie took a deep breath. "I might be later, Mom. I have some other things to do."

"Things? Things?" she said shrilly. "Julie, unless you can be more specific, I will expect you at two."

There were a million excuses she could have made—having lunch with Megan, going to the library, visiting Springhill. But she would have choked on another lie. "Would two-thirty be okay?" She could see Loretta and Bagley for two hours and be back by then.

Her mother nodded. "Not a minute later." She was still hurt, Julie could tell.

When the bus pulled into Potatoville, Julie's heart lifted. Nothing had changed. She got off the bus and looked down Penny Lane. Three little kids and a big orange dog ran through a lawn sprinkler, woofing and shrieking and falling over one another in excitement. A teenage boy in cut-offs was bent over a lawnmower, pulling the start cord over and over. Each time the mower would rev loudly for a few seconds, then sputter out. The smell of fried potatoes drifted through the air. Lunch at Ike's, Julie thought, heading down the sidewalk toward Loretta's. As she got closer to the house, she thought of Winston bounding out to greet her. As if on cue, he came charging around the side of the big white house, his tail whipping the air.

"Winston," Julie yelled, putting her arms around his shaggy neck and laughing as he poked his nose in her face. "You are more powerful than a speeding locomotive, Winston. No wonder you gave me nightmares." Grabbing his collar, she tugged him up to the front door. The doorbell had been broken since April, so she knocked and pushed open the door.

"Loretta! Bagley!" Nobody was at the phone lines. In fact, Julie couldn't even see the telephones. They were hidden behind stacks of dishes, left over from the yard sale. She recognized the pale gold and green vine pattern; some of her grandma's knickknacks were also scattered over the table. Loretta was probably going to take the stuff to Sammy the Pawner some day, Julie thought. But why wasn't she answering the phones?

As if it had been waiting for her arrival, a phone rang. Julie poked around the table, pushing plates and cups aside. She squatted down and found the ringing phone under one of the folding chairs. "The Queen of Dreamland." She stood up and made a spot for the phone on the table. "Would you like to tell me your dream?"

"Who's this?"

Julie looked around for Loretta, or even Mrs. Og. "The Queen of Dreamland," she repeated. "Who's this?"

"Arthur. You sound different." He went on without pausing. "In my dream I'm all different pieces—bones, heart, lungs, brain. And all these pieces are in different drawers in this spick-and-span room, all white, see?"

Cramp walked into the room, stooping because Bagley was on his shoulders.

"Bagley!" Julie shouted into the phone.

"Beg pardon?"

"Oops, sorry, Arthur. Go ahead." She blew kisses at Bagley while Cramp positioned him below the tail of the American Beauty kite that was taped to the ceiling. While Arthur told her about all his pieces being stitched together by a lady in a silver dress, she watched Bagley tug the kite, and some of the plaster, off the ceiling.

"She did a good job," Arthur said. "You can hardly see the stitches. It's not like I'm some kind of Frankenstein or anything."

"That's a very positive dream," Julie said, recalling what she had read about sewing in Loretta's dream book. "It means your life is going to come together at last."

"Do you mean what I think you mean?"

"Well . . . yes," Julie said, anxious to end the conversation and talk to Bagley.

Arthur whooped into the phone and hung up.

"Hi, Bagley! Hi, Cramp! Where's Loretta?"

Cramp lifted Bagley off his shoulders and settled him in the bean-bag chair.

"We don't know," Bagley answered cheerfully. "She left us a note, didn't she, Cramp?"

Instead of answering, Cramp disappeared down the hallway.

"Here." Bagley took a note from the pocket of his shorts. He smoothed it out against his thigh. " 'Dear Bagley and Cramp,' " he read in his thin voice, " 'Mrs. Og is visiting her girlfriend and I'm out for a lark! You are in charge of the phones. See you. xoxoxoxoxoxo, Loretta.' "

Julie got up and looked at the note in Bagley's lap. "No phone number?"

Cramp came back down the hall, wearing a black beret pulled down over his bad ear. He was pushing Bagley's wheelchair. Julie repeated the question.

Cramp shook his head. "Just the note." He picked up Bagley and put him in the wheelchair, his tall, muscled frame bent down so that his ponytail dipped over his shoulder. "You still want to go watch Bad Howard in the ring?" he said softly to Bagley.

Bagley looked from Cramp to Julie and shook his head. "Not today, Cramp. Would you get me his autograph?"

"Are you leaving?" Julie asked, even though Cramp never wore his black beret unless he was going out. "You're not going to answer the phones?"

Cramp flashed a rare smile, showing his gold tooth. "I'm out for a lark, too, Missy." And he was gone.

The phone rang again. Julie stared at it.

"Aren't you going to answer it?" Bagley asked.

On the fourth ring, Julie picked up. "The Queen of Dreamland is out for a lark," she said. And hung up.

Bagley started giggling but Julie didn't. She threw herself into the beanbag chair and groaned. "I came over here for a lark, too. Not to answer the stupid phones. If Dreamland is so important to Loretta, why doesn't she stay home and answer them herself?"

Bagley stopped laughing. "Are you mad at her?"

"What she does with her life is her business. Is she out with that—with Duane again?"

Bagley shrugged. "Probably."

Julie *was* mad. Her life was a mess. Her mother was upset with her. She had lied for the umpteenth time so she could sneak over here and Loretta wasn't even here. On top of that, Loretta assumed that other people would take care of Bagley and answer the dreamlines. And she didn't tell anyone where she was. Just— "I'm out for a lark." Julie felt rejected, like Loretta had purposefully turned her back on her. She wondered if Bagley felt the same way.

"Are you mad about anything?" she asked him carefully.

Bagley laughed. "You're here, Jewel. How could I be mad?"

Julie blinked. She felt like Bagley had hit her over the head with a board. "I'm such a shmuck, Bagley."

"How come?"

"I have this dummy at home, this mannequin, you know?"

He nodded. "Like they put in store windows with clothes on?"

"Right. I dragged her out of a Dumpster four years ago and named her Jacquelina and dressed her in my clothes and kept her in my bedroom. I even used to sleep with her every night. You know why?"

"Cuz you're a smuk?"

She laughed. "No, because I wanted a little sister or a little brother."

"Ha!" Bagley pressed his hands to his chest. "Like me."

Julie nodded. "But I never really thought I'd ever have a real live one. Especially one with gray eyes and blond hair, who can make wonderful kites out of just sticks and paper. And who"—she raised a finger and poked him in the chest— "has a heart made out of cotton candy."

Bagley flapped his hand at her. "Aw, Jewel, you *are* a smuk."

"No, Bagley, it's true. If your heart were a kite, it would fly straight up to heaven."

"Hey!" Bagley reached down and picked up his kite. "Jewel, could we go out and fly it? There's an empty field next door without any trees. Could we?"

The phone rang again. Julie grinned at Bagley as she picked it up. "The Queen of Dreamland is out flying a kite," she said and hung up.

She carried the kite, following Winston and Bagley down the hall. Winston pushed open the screen door and held it open with his body while Julie pushed Bagley over the threshold and out onto the back porch. The wheels clattered over the bare, creaky boards as she pushed Bagley's chair toward the ramp Cramp had built for him at the far end. She paused for a moment, pushing Bagley up next to the old wooden slats so they could enjoy the shade of the wide, covered porch.

Even though it was a hot day, the old porch was cool, and a little breeze lifted Julie's hair off her neck. She looked out over the yard, at the broken cement sidewalk below and the beds of daisies and black-eyed Susans all choked with weeds. A garden like this would be her mother's worst nightmare but it could be pretty with a little work, she thought. If she could get Cramp to repair the loose boards in the porch and fix the sidewalk, she could paint and weed and plant new flowers. "I like it back here," she said to Bagley.

"Yeah." He nodded. "Someday I'm going to climb that tree."

Together they looked at a huge, old maple that spread over most of the backyard. "After your operation," Julie said, "you'll climb lots of trees."

"And I'll have lots of friends," he added.

Julie flushed with anger. "What kind of pinheads won't be your friend just because you can't walk?"

Bagley shook his head. "It doesn't matter one bit, Jewel. Because I'm going to walk very very soon."

Julie thought about the five hundred forty-seven dollars from the yard sale and how many dollars they had to go to reach seventeen thousand. "Of course you are." She picked up the kite again. "Let's see if this thing can fly."

Around the corner of the house came a big, orange dog chasing a squirrel. Winston jumped to his feet and growled.

"Easy, killer," Julie said, grabbing his collar. But it was too late. Winston lunged at the side of the porch, knocking down a six-foot section of railing, and went leaping down into the yard. Julie hung onto Winston's collar a second too long and followed him over the side, taking Bagley's wheelchair with her.

Julie sailed head over heels and landed on her rear, her hands smacking down on a hill of pinecones. Behind her, she heard Bagley's wheelchair hit the cement and clatter and bang and crash. Julie lifted herself gingerly, brushing her hands against her shorts. "Bagley," she called turning around and stepping over the smashed kite.

Bagley had fallen free of the wheelchair onto the broken sidewalk. His legs stuck straight up against a big bush like two white sticks. He didn't move.

"Bagley!" she shouted, diving down beside him. She looked at his still, white face, his eyes shut, glasses broken and realized he had struck his head. "Oh, God," she cried, pulling him onto her lap. "Bagley, are you all right?" She took off his broken glasses and laid them in the grass.

"Winston!" she called desperately. Winston bounded back from his brief fling and stood next to her, looking down at Bagley. "Oh, Winston, we've got to do something." But she sat there, petrified, not having the slightest idea what to do. She looked at Bagley's face, as pale and reposed as a statue, and she turned away. She couldn't bear to see him like that—like he was dead. She heard a faint moan and she looked again. Bagley's eyelids fluttered slightly. "Oh, Winston." She lifted her face to the dog who was now whining and leaping back and forth over Bagley's body. "He's okay, Winston. He's not dead. We've got to get him in the house."

She slid one arm under Bagley's neck and raised herself on one knee to get her other arm under his knees. With Winston running in furious circles around her and barking wildly, Julie managed to get to her feet. "It's okay," she whispered to Bagley. "Jewel has you, Bagley. I'm going to take care of you now." Talking nonstop, she carried him up the ramp while Winston nosed open the screen and held it for her.

"It's all right, Bagley," she kept saying as they made their way down the hall. She was talking to herself as much as she was talking to Bagley, trying to calm her racing heart, trying to figure out what to do. There wasn't a sofa in the living room so Julie squatted and lay him down on the rag rug between the beanbags. She grabbed an old velveteen pillow and slid it under his head. Then, even though it was sweltering, she jumped up and got the red-fringed shawl off the dining-room table and tucked it around him, because people in accidents were always covered.

"Bagley," she whispered, leaning over him. His eyelids flickered open and he looked at Julie. She was so relieved she laughed out loud. "Hey, Bagley Wagley! Are you okay now? I mean, you didn't break any bones, did you? Or anything?"

But Bagley didn't answer. He just stared as if she was a stone wall.

"Just point," Julie pleaded. "Point to where it hurts." She took his warm little hand from under the red shawl and squeezed it. She thought of all the times she had counted the sections of blue glass in the church windows when she should have been praying. "Please, God," she whispered, "I never thought I'd ever have a little brother that I loved so much. I don't care if he ever walks again. I just want him to be like he was. I'm sorry for all the lies but please don't punish Bagley. Please make him well and I promise I'll tell the truth. I'll tell everyone the truth."

She could feel the pulse in Bagley's fingers, feel the blood running beneath his skin. Maybe she couldn't help him. And neither could Cramp, nor Mrs. Og, nor even Loretta. But she knew someone who could.

When her mother answered the phone, the words came out in a rush. "Mom, I need you—come as fast as you can. I'm alone in this house with Bagley and he's hurt—Mom, he's really hurt bad and he can't talk anymore." Then she started to cry.

"Julie? For heaven's sake, what are you talking about? Where are you? Are you all right?"

Julie yelled into the phone. "Don't keep asking questions! Just come! Seventy-eight Penny Lane in Potatoville. Hurry." She slammed down the receiver.

17

The waiting was worse than her worst nightmare. Julie's teeth started to chatter and she felt like she was going to throw up. She sat on the floor next to Bagley and took his hand. "My mother is coming," she said, trying to sound calm. "She's coming right now." She took a deep breath and tried to picture her mother hurrying to get out the door. "She has her purse in her hand, Bagley, and she's finding her car keys. Now she's going out the back door into the garage. Remember, like you did that day with Loretta? When it was raining?" she said anxiously. "The day you made all the ice stars?" She leaned over and looked into Bagley's face. His eyes were still closed, almost as if he was asleep. But his face didn't look peaceful. It was tight and his lips were pinched, like something was hurting him.

"She's very good with hurts, Bagley. She's a good, good lady, you'll see. Once when I tore my toenail off at Marvin's Dock, she piggybacked me forty-three steps up to the cottage where the Band-Aids were. And she's not that young, Bagley, not like Loretta. But she has a good heart. She's great at taking care of people. Now, she's driving down Dalrymple Street, speeding like a maniac. I sure hope she doesn't get a speeding ticket, don't you?"

In between her chatter, Julie felt little stabs of fear over what was going to happen when her mother came into Loretta's house and learned the truth. "It doesn't matter," she said, holding Bagley's hand against her cheek. "All that matters is you, Bagley. My mom will fix you up. She might be old and kind of fat but she's excellent at fixing people. I've been sick a million times, a trillion times and every time she took care of me. Sometimes if I had a bad dream she'd sit up and sing to me till I fell back asleep." Julie took a deep breath and started singing in a shaky voice:

Fly little baby, fly to the sky
Fly to the angels singing on high.
Fall little baby, fall to my arms
For I will keep you safe from all harms.

Winston tucked his nose under his paws and whimpered from under the table. It was all he could do. And singing was all Julie could do. The familiar words calmed her a little. She imagined her mother racing to get to her, speeding through the streets, around corners, past the Dairy Queen, the Family Video, and the Holy Childhood Day Care Center where all the toddlers went out walking, one behind the other, holding onto a rope, like toy ducks. "Fall to my arms—"

There was a quick sound at the door, and then Mrs. Solus rushed into the room. She stood there staring for a moment before Winston leaped. It was from relief, Julie was sure—the same relief she felt when she saw her mother, the person who could help Bagley. As he sprang, Winston snagged the leg of the rickety table and everything—all the china plates and cups and fussy little statues went flying, sending up a wild cacophony to mark this wild and perilous moment in the lives of the three people in the room.

Forgetting Bagley and the broken china behind her, Julie

screamed and tore at Winston. Her mother screamed in concert, clutching her purse and falling back against the door. Grabbing the first thing she could lay her hands on, a phone book, Julie smacked Winston across the nose, sending him whimpering off into a corner.

"He's okay, Mom. He won't hurt you, I promise." Julie put her arms around her mother and drew her back into the room. "Be calm, be calm, Mom. Just cool down and don't worry about Winston. Just let's be calm," she repeated.

"Oh my lord, Julie," her mother sputtered. "What is going on? What is going on? You call me. I have a hair appointment at three. This place, this awful place. And that dog, that horrible—" Mrs. Solus stopped when she saw Bagley. "What's wrong? Your little friend from the park?" She dropped her purse and knelt on the floor, putting her hand on Bagley's forehead. He opened his eyes.

Winston leaped up again and started barking.

"Shut up!" Julie yelled over her shoulder. "Shut up, you stupid dog. You're just making things worse."

There was another sound at the door. This time it was Loretta who swept into the room, wearing a coronet of flowers in her hair. "Judas H. Priest, what's wrong? What's happened to Bagley? Out of my way." She pushed Julie's mother aside and took Bagley's face in her hands. "What's wrong with my baby? Jewel," she said, not taking her eyes off Bagley's face, "tell me quick, Jewel."

"He fell," Julie said breathlessly, "off the back porch. He hit his head, I think. He . . . he . . . he c-can't t-t-talk anymore." Julie could scarcely talk herself. She was so frightened for Bagley and suddenly equally frightened for herself. Julie's mother was staring at Loretta, but Loretta seemed oblivious.

"Bagley!" she screamed, cradling his head in her hands.

The gray eyes flickered open and Bagley looked at her. "What?" he whispered. "Why are you yelling?"

"Ooh," Loretta said, drawing Bagley close to her chest. "Thank God."

"Thank God," Julie echoed, sinking into a beanbag.

Except for Loretta's soft crooning, the room was silent. Julie's mother looked from Loretta to Julie, then back at Loretta. But she said nothing.

Julie had the overpowering feeling that this moment, this entire situation, was a strange dream. Her mother, her sweet, gentle mother, was the only mother she had ever known. And as soon as she woke up, Loretta, Bagley, this house and everything in it, would be lifted up and carried out of her mind like Dorothy's house in Kansas. She suddenly ached to be home in her own bed with her mother singing her a little sleep song.

Julie's mother had moved away from Loretta, her attention caught by the fallen table and the china wreckage. "Those plates." Her voice sounded strange to Julie's ear. It had an emotion in it she couldn't name. Her mother must be amazed, Julie thought, to see her grandmother's plates broken on the floor of this strange house. But the task of explaining was too much for her. It had nothing to do with her grandmother's plates.

"What does this mean?" Her mother stooped over and picked up a broken cup, a half cup with the gold and green vine cut off where the break was.

Julie's mother moved toward Loretta, who was crouched beside Bagley on the floor. Loretta was chatting away as if nothing had happened. And Bagley was talking now, talking quietly. She must have seen Mrs. Solus standing there right at her elbow but Loretta didn't look up until Mrs. Solus said, in a strange, quivering voice, "What are you doing here?"

Julie blinked. Her mother didn't say, "Who are you?" She didn't say, "What are these plates doing in your house?" The way she said it was unfriendly, as if Loretta didn't belong in her own house.

"I live here," Loretta said, flipping back her hair, not looking up. "Me and Bagley."

"What," Mrs. Solus asked, holding out the broken cup like she wanted Loretta to fill it up, "are you doing with my daughter?"

Ignoring her, Loretta said to Bagley, "Do you feel like sitting up? Where's your wheelchair?"

"Oh." Julie raised her hand. "It's outside still. I'll go get it." She jumped up.

"You'd better stay here, Julie." Her mother shot her a look.

"We could put you in a beanbag," Loretta coaxed.

Bagley nodded.

"Jewel? Could you help me, hon?"

Julie slunk past her mother and helped lift Bagley into a chair. "How's your head?" she whispered.

"Hurts," he whispered back.

"What are you doing with my daughter?" Mrs. Solus said again, her words as sharp as the edge of a knife.

When Loretta turned around and pushed up the sleeves of her vibrant purple dress, Julie noticed she was wearing Julie's brooch in her hair along with the ring of purple flowers. For the first time since she met her, Julie wished that Loretta dressed differently, more like her mother, in navy blue pantsuits and button-down-the-front dresses. In her skinny purple heels Loretta looked cheap.

"I'm getting reacquainted with her," Loretta said, looking Mrs. Solus in the eye this time. "My daughter," she said deliberately.

Julie tensed. Loretta could be such a bulldog. Why didn't she break it to her gently? She glanced at her poor mother, ready to catch her if she fainted. But her mother's face had turned scarlet. She looked madder than Julie had ever seen her.

"I told you—we both told you—to stay away from Julie. That was a trust, Loretta, a solemn trust. Not something to be broken on a whim. We certainly didn't expect you to follow us to this town, to move here, so you could track her down, ensnare her—"

"Ensnare her?" Loretta shrieked. "Ensnare my own daughter? Lay a trap for my own daughter? What crap. Jewel loves coming here. She loves us, me and Bagley." She looked past Mrs. Solus. "Did I lay a trap for you or what, Jewel?"

Julie stared openmouthed at Loretta and her mother. "What?" she said blankly. "Do you know each other?"

"Well, I guess the picture-perfect mother forgot to tell you, didn't she?" Loretta said, putting her hands on her hips.

Her mother said, "Julie, I'm sorry you've been dragged into this. I wish I knew just what had been going on here. It's unfortunate that you got involved with this woman, but this is going to stop right this minute."

"No!" Loretta shouted.

Her mother turned in a fury. "How dare you?"

"No!" echoed Julie. All the years of being led by her mother, told that she must wear her hair a certain way, that she mustn't put catsup on pot roast, or speak to strangers, gathered like an angry storm in her chest. Her mother was no longer in charge. This wasn't about pot roast. It was Julie's life.

"Julie—" Her mother put her hands out to her. "Julie, you've been misled, can't you see, darling? This woman connived to get in touch with you and then she took advantage. These plates, your grandmother's plates—"

"I gave them to her!" Julie bellowed. "I gave them to her!"

"And that brooch, Julie. It's worth a great deal. She knew that, don't you see? Even if you didn't."

"Take it—" Loretta yanked the brooch from her hair and threw it at Mame's feet.

"No," Julie sobbed. She stumbled forward and picked up the brooch. "Please, Loretta, I want you to have it."

Loretta crossed her arms over her chest. "I don't want it, Jewel. I don't want anything from you that your—MOM—doesn't want me to have."

"Wait." Her mother took the brooch from Julie and held it out to Loretta. "I've changed my mind. I do want you to have this, Loretta. I think you want it, don't you? And it . . . it's worth a lot of money. Sell it if you want to. Or just wear it. It looks lovely in your hair."

Loretta turned to her, eyes narrowed. "Oh yeah?"

"Please, let's forget all these hasty words, Loretta. Let's forget everything. All I want is for you to forget Julie. Forget you ever saw her."

"Ha!" Loretta spit the word in Mame's face. "Ha, ha, ha. That old trick again. It might have worked fourteen years ago, but it's not going down today."

Julie looked from her mother to Loretta. There was something between them, something she didn't understand. She had never seen her mother act this way, so angry, so afraid. What did Loretta mean? Some awful awareness started to open inside her. All those years her mother wouldn't talk. She was keeping something from Julie. Loretta, too.

"What old trick?" Julie said. "What are you talking about?"

"Nothing, Julie," her mother replied in that so irritating, so familiar voice that said to Julie that it was something all right, but not something for her to know. "I think we should go now," Mrs. Solus said icily. "You'll want to have your little boy checked by a doctor, I expect. He may have a concussion." She clicked her purse open, dropped in the brooch, and shut it. A sign to Julie.

"No," Bagley said anxiously. "Don't go, Jewel."

Julie didn't budge. "Loretta? What old trick?"

Loretta looked at the floor, tugging at her hair.

Julie stared. Loretta had never dodged a question from her before. "Loretta, not you. Please—don't you lie to me, too. I don't care what it is. Just tell me."

Loretta shook her head. "I can't, Jewel." She looked up at Julie, her face tight and afraid. "I can't."

The room was silent. Julie could hear the steady drip of the faucet. Outside, a dog barked. She wondered if it was the orange one who had caused so much trouble. She wished with all her heart she had never seen that orange dog, never heard what she was about to hear. "Did you sell me?" Julie said to Loretta in a voice as dry as dust.

Loretta clutched at her throat and shook her head. "It wasn't like that, Jewel. Not like that at all, hon. See—they offered the money. I didn't ask for it. I never would have asked for it."

"Julie—" Her mother put her arms around her and tried to hold her close.

Julie pulled away. "How much?" she said to her mother. "How much was I worth to you?"

Her mother shook her head. "There's no price tag on you, Julie," she said in a trembling voice.

"Shit," Loretta said. "You might as well tell her, Mame. What's the point of another lie? Ten thousand," she said. "Ten thousand for me and fourteen years of heartbreak."

18

Julie sat in the window seat of her room staring out at the evening sky. Through the open window came a breeze, chilly for late August. But she barely noticed the cold seeping through her thin cotton pajamas. The water below reflected the colors of the sunset—lavender and pink and gold—broken here and there by the shadows of the poplars. She imagined the pool was a small lake in a distant woods where deer came to drink, the only sound the cry of a blackbird overhead. A life in a cabin on a small lake alone—that was what she longed for. With a dog to lie down with in front of the fireplace while the wind howled outside. Finally Julie noticed the chill and leaned forward to crank the window shut. She drew her legs up under her chin and looked at Jacquelina, sitting there in the shadows looking back at her.

"What would you do?" she whispered across the window seat. "If you were set adrift in a wooden boat without any oars? And the shore was a thousand miles away? And you had no food? And no—" She sighed and closed her eyes, leaning against the cool window. After a few minutes she looked up. "You stupid dummy. You never told me one thing in my whole life."

She swung off the window seat, grabbed her gray sweatshirt out of a dresser drawer, and pulled it on. Then her tennies. She picked up Jacquelina and started downstairs.

"Where do you think you're going at this time of night?" her mother said, coming from the living room. Her parents had been talking in low tones, but had stopped when they heard Julie on the stairs.

"I'm going to throw Jacquelina back in the Dumpster," Julie said bluntly.

"In the Dumpster? But, Julie," her mother sputtered, "that's silly, darling. Why? You've had her for years, poor old thing. She's not doing any harm. Maybe, maybe—the church sewing circle could use her. For fittings?"

Julie shook her head. "She's a stupid overgrown baby doll." She started for the door, hoisting Jacquelina over her shoulder and holding her by one leg.

"You're wearing pajamas!" her mother gasped. "Julie, come back here and change. Wayne, come and talk some sense into her."

But Julie didn't stop. She went out the door and down the sidewalk, lifting her face to the fading colors of the night, hurrying because she might change her mind. She walked two blocks to Baskerson's Drugstore. She smiled and said hello when she passed Mrs. Merriwether, the president of her mother's rose garden club, just as if she was on her way to school. And she was glad when Mrs. Merriwether looked down and saw her pajama bottoms.

Julie lifted the lid of the Dumpster behind Baskerson's. The smells of sour milk and rotting newsprint rose to her nostrils. A streetlight from Washington Street lit its black emptiness like the inside of a cave. Lifting Jacquelina, Julie slid her down the metal sides until she hit bottom and fell over. "Good-bye, Jacquelina," she whispered. She stared down into the Dumpster for a long moment and then let go of the lid. She ran as fast as she could all the way home.

Her mother and father were waiting for her. "We'd like to talk with you," her father said. "Come into the living room."

Julie followed them, knowing they were going to say the same things, the very same things they had been saying for weeks.

Her mother and father sat side by side on the rose tapestry love seat; Julie sat across the room from them on the piano bench. Her father scratched his head. "Mother and I—we're worried about you, Julie. You're just not yourself these days. Not talking to us, spending all your time up in your room listening to music. And now this—throwing your doll, Jacqueline, whatever her name is, into the Dumpster." He leaned forward and spread his hands on the coffee table. "Now we know this thing a few weeks ago upset you, and I—"

"It wasn't a thing, Dad," Julie said icily.

"Oh, darling, you're right," her mother rushed in. "We had no right to deceive you about your past. We just didn't think it was that important. The important thing was that you were our daughter and that we loved you—love you—so very much."

"People who love you don't make up lies about you, about the most important part of your life."

"Don't forget" —Her father lifted a finger— "you deceived us as well. All those times you went over there."

Julie wanted to leap to her feet and scream. Her father had some nerve comparing her lies to his and her mother's. She had only done what anyone in her position would do—see her natural mother, the person she'd been longing to see her whole life. The person who held the answers to the entire mystery of her being, who she'd dreamed about since she was old enough to remember her dreams. But she couldn't say it. She couldn't say anything about Loretta. Because what

Loretta had done was worst of all. She stared at her tennies and muttered, "It wasn't the same."

Julie let them go on, fumbling over the same ground, making excuses, apologizing.

"I'm not ashamed," her father said at last. "I would have given a hundred thousand dollars for you. A million, if I'd had it. We couldn't wait, Julie, don't you see? We were forty-two years old. The babies were going to the young couples in their twenties and thirties. Not to couples whose hair was turning gray." He tried a joke. "What I had of it."

Finally she stood up. "Maybe that's true. Maybe everything you say is true. But it's all changed now between us. It changes everything."

"But, but, darling—" Her mother rose from the sofa.

"I can't explain it," Julie said. "I'm not who I thought I was and neither are you. I'm going to bed."

Up in her room, Julie dragged out the stuffed animals from under the dresser and filled the empty window seat. Then she flopped across the bed. She was glad Jacquelina was gone. Fourteen-year-olds didn't play with dolls, she thought. And that was what she was—a fourteen-year-old with a make-believe little girl. Pretending she had a sweet little sister was like pretending she had a wonderful fantasy mother who had pined for her all her life and then come back to find her.

Whenever she thought of Loretta, a hardness came around her heart like a big metal fence. She rolled over and picked up her headphones to shut out the feeling. Her eye caught the blinking red light of her answering machine. She hit the button.

"Jewel, hon, I can't live like this. My heart is fairly breaking in two. You're being cruel to not at least talk to me, Jewel. Listen to me," Loretta wailed. "Don't you think I know it was wrong? Not taking the money so much as giving you up. Oh, taking the money was wrong, too. I'm not saying it was right. But giving you up, Jewel, was the worst mistake of my life. Did you hear me, Jewel? I tried to trade back again but they wouldn't listen. I always wanted you back. There was never a time when I didn't grieve over you. Gospel, Jewel, gospel." There was a pause. "Hon, Bagley loved it when you talked with him. Listen now, I'm going to put him back on, J—"

Julie pushed the stop button and hit rewind. She could just barely tolerate listening to Loretta, but listening to Bagley was like a knife in the heart. One time he caught her and she couldn't hang up on him.

"Are you still mad at us?" he had asked her.

"I'm not mad at you, Bagley," she had answered. But she didn't mince words. "It's Loretta I'm mad at."

"Because she sold you for ten thousand dollars?"

"That," Julie said, "and because she lied."

"She said she didn't sell you?"

"She—not exactly—she just let me believe that she gave me to my parents. Like a present."

"I don't see what you're mad about. Ten thousand dollars is a lot of money. I wish I was worth ten thousand dollars."

Julie almost smiled. "You're worth a lot more than that, Bagley."

"I know," he said, breaking into giggles.

How could he still be the same? she wondered. Not choosing sides, not mad at anyone. Was it because he still trusted grown-ups?

One day during the first week of school Julie's father had pulled up to the curb to let her off when she spotted a blue truck across the street with a wheelchair in the back. "Dad," she said, getting back in the car, "Could you let me off at the other entrance today?" She didn't see them anymore after that.

Another two weeks passed and Julie was back in her school routine, slaving over algebra, trying to remember the names of the Spanish explorers. She ate lunch with Megan every day now, just as she had before Charlie. One day, sitting in the lunch room, eating an egg salad sandwich while Megan polished her nails, it struck her with a piercing sadness that life was going on the same as before. The maple leaves were just starting to get tinged with red. Big black V's of geese had started their southern journeys. Over by the juice machine, boys blew up their lunch bags and popped them like they had every year since first grade. The world didn't care about her sadness, she thought. Life went on.

At home after school she sat at the piano and thought about the song she had written for Loretta. She would never sing it again. It was as if Loretta had never happened. Or Bagley. They were gone from her life and she was left with a pain in her heart that would never heal. What was the point of it all? It would have been better to never know about them. To believe to the end of her days that she was given to her parents by a pink fairy. She sighed and then changed her mind. No, there had been too many lies in her life. At least she had learned that.

She poised her hands above the keyboard, waiting for inspiration. A gasp came from the library, where her mother was going through more boxes from her grandma's house.

"Julie, come look at this," her mother called.

Julie got up from the bench and went to the library, where she found her mother surrounded by tissue paper and cardboard. She was holding an old doll.

"Look," she said, lifting it up for Julie to see. It was a baby doll with a shiny wooden face and glass eyes that opened and shut. Her long cotton nightie was gray with age. "This was mine," she said. "She must be over fifty years old. Annie Louey." She smiled down at the doll. "My mother bought her for me the first Christmas we were together again. Oh, Annie Louey," she whispered, gently stroking the thin mat of yellow hair. "I haven't held you in such a long time."

Julie watched her mother's fingers fuss with the old nightgown, smoothing out the wrinkles. She cradled Annie Louey in her arms and started to rock back and forth on the leather sofa. Julie looked away.

"Here." Her mother held the doll out to her. "I want you to have her."

Julie shook her head.

"Please," her mother said. "Please take her, Julie."

"I don't want your old doll," Julie said thickly. Tears sprang to her eyes and it made her angry. "Stupid doll," she said, putting her hands in her back jeans pockets.

Her mother got up then, tugged at Julie's arms and put the doll into them.

Before Julie knew it, she was wrapping her arms around Annie Louey and tucking her head down to Annie Louey's head. Tears ran down her cheeks and onto Annie Louey's matted yellow hair. All the tears that she had been carrying inside her poured out like she had been tipped upside down.

Julie's mother wrapped her arms around Julie and Annie Louey and rocked them back and forth in the middle of the floor. "Why did you throw Jacquelina away?" she whispered into Julie's hair.

"Because," Julie stammered. "Because she was, she—she—I hated her," she blurted out. The words came boiling out of her, too fast to think. "She was me—I was throwing myself away. All I deserve is to crawl around in the bottom of a dirty old Dumpster. I hate myself! I'm ugly, I'm a mean, dishonest person and everybody else hates me, too. I snuck away every Saturday and didn't go visit Grandma and she died and now I'll never ever get to see her again." She hiccuped and wiped her nose on her sleeve. "I know you'll never forgive me for that. And you didn't want me to go see my birth mother and you were right about that, too. She couldn't wait to get rid of me when I was born. She sold me like a slab of bacon. All those years I was growing up I wondered if she really might love me. But now I know. She hates me. She lied to me. She pretended to like me but she was lying!"

"Come here." Her mother led Julie to the sofa. "Sit here and listen to me." She set Annie Louey beside her and took Julie's hands. "Darling, we lied to you as well."

"I know," Julie sniffed. "You hate me, too."

"Do you really believe that?" Her mother tipped Julie's face up to look in her eyes.

Julie gazed at the worn, familiar face, that face that, for fourteen years, had looked at Julie as if she were dropped from heaven. She shook her head ever so slightly.

Her mother sighed and looked away. "All those years, Julie, all those years of trying to have a baby, wanting so desperately, you can't imagine. Once, I got pregnant and your father and I were so excited. It was like we had hit the Irish Sweepstakes. He went around passing out cigars—that's how silly he was. And then it was over. I—just lost it. All our hopes were dashed. Until someone—a person who went to our church mentioned this young girl in another town who had no money, no place to stay, and she was going to have a baby."

"Loretta?"

Her mother nodded. "One weekend we drove to see her, offered to pay her medical bills, pay for a place for her to stay if we could adopt her baby." She hesitated. "We—we didn't offer her money."

Julie had been listening quietly, stroking Annie Louey in her lap. She looked up. "You didn't?"

Her mother shook her head. "We signed the papers at the hospital. And we brought you, this beautiful miracle baby, home as our very own."

So far it sounded like a pretty ordinary adoption, Julie thought. Sign papers. Bring the baby home.

"But Loretta came back."

Julie blinked. "What?"

"She changed her mind. Mothers who give their babies up can do that. They have thirty days to change their mind."

Julie's heart started pounding in her chest. "She wanted me back?"

"Yes." Her mother nodded.

"And . . ." Julie hesitated. She drew in a long shuddering breath. "That's when you offered her money. Ten thousand dollars."

"Yes," her mother said again very softly. "We would have given her all we had."

Julie nodded. She felt like someone had taken an ax to her heart.

Her mother went on. "We told Loretta that the only condition of the money was that she get out of our lives forever and never, ever try to contact you. And then, one week later, we moved away. To Canopy."

"Why?" Julie asked. "If she took the money and agreed never to see me?"

Her mother let out a piteous little cry. "Because I knew she would come back for you. I saw her face, Julie. And it was the face of an old, broken woman who had seen her baby die before her eyes. She loved you, Julie. She loved you and couldn't have you. But we loved you, too, and we had something she didn't."

"Money," Julie whispered.

"In a way, darling, I've never forgiven myself. It was the cruelest act I've ever committed against another human being. And as much as I've feared her, I have grieved for Loretta, too. For the last fourteen years."

Julie got up. Still holding Annie Louey she left the room.

19

It was the middle of October. Julie sat on the front porch in her red beret, looking at the sky. There was no chair, no wooden swing on the porch, only the hard, rectangular, cream-colored brick to sit on. After a short while, the front door opened. Her mother, wrapped in her father's sweater against the chilly morning, eased herself down beside Julie.

"You're up early for a Saturday morning," she said, handing Julie a cup of hot chocolate.

Julie nodded. She sipped the hot chocolate and looked back at the sky.

"Ohhh," her mother said, seeing what Julie was looking at. "The geese."

Looking above the golden crown of the birch tree at the corner of the drive, they watched the geese move like the point of an arrow through the geranium-colored sky. After a few minutes, her mother said, "They make me think of things I have to do. Those geese, they're always on schedule. Every year I see them and every year I think of the things I haven't done. The pool has to be drained. I have to dig up my bulbs. Your father has to take down the screens." She shook her head. "I seem to be falling further behind." She sighed. "Your mother's getting old, Julie."

Julie looked at her, looked at her mother's lined face, her saggy eyes. She wanted to comfort her, tell her that she was still young, but she was having the same kind of thoughts. The geese reminded her that time was rushing by. Back in July, she had wanted time to pass, to erase the sharp pain in her heart, the hollow feeling in her stomach. But now that October was here, with golden leaves skittering through the air and football games every Friday night, the geese were just another sign that life was going on without her. She was outside the great turning wheel of the seasons, of falling leaves and southbound geese. She was still caught in July, trying to unravel the great mystery of her life.

"Would you look at that pink sky?" her mother said. "My mother used to wait for a pink sky to dig up her bulbs because she knew it would be overcast. Well, that's a sign," she said, slapping her knees. "I'll do it today. You can help me, Julie. You can do the area around the birdbath."

Julie put the cup of cocoa on the step between them. She leaned forward, hugging her knees, and watched a squirrel running across the lawn with an acorn in its mouth. After the squirrel disappeared around the forsythia, Julie spoke. "There's something I have to do, too." She turned and looked at her mother.

For a moment her mother didn't say a word. She rolled up the sleeves of her sweater, three rolls on each sleeve, exactly the same. Then she rolled them down again and folded her hands in her lap. "You're going to see her."

"I have to, Mom. I can't just let her go. She means too much to never see her again."

Her mother tried to speak. Then she shook her head and looked away, down the street to where a neighbor in a baseball cap was raking leaves. He waved. Mame didn't see him. She wiped a tear from one eye, then the other. Finally, she said, "I didn't mean to hurt you, Julie. I thought I was protecting you all these years."

She gave a bitter laugh. "Now I see it was me I was protecting. If you didn't know about her, about Loretta, I thought you wouldn't care. That you wouldn't even think about that other person in your life. And you would be our little girl forever. Nobody else's. Of course you cared. How could you not care? She gave birth to you. She was your mother." She gave a long, shuddering sigh. "Oh, Julie, I'm sorry. I'm just a foolish old woman, aren't I?"

"Yes, Mom." Julie stood up. "Mom?"

"Umm?" Her mother looked at her.

"I love you."

Her mother got up and put her arms around Julie. They stood there holding each other in the quiet October morning as though Julie were leaving for a long, treacherous journey.

Julie pulled away. "See you later, Mom." She walked down the sidewalk and across the street to the corner of Larch where the bus stopped. Just before she got on, she looked back. Her mother was still standing there.

The bus driver remembered her. "Been a while," he said, pushing the lever to release her quarters. They tinkled into the box. "Still taking those piano lessons?"

The way he said it, out of the corner of his mouth, it sounded like "peeaner lessons." Julie shook her head and moved to a seat.

"That's no way to get to Carnegie Hall," he said, stepping on the gas. "Feller gets on the bus and asks me," he called over his shoulder, 'How do I get to Carnegie Hall?' I tell him, 'Practice, man, practice.'"

He laughed all the way to the next stop but Julie was too nervous to laugh. She didn't know what she was going to say to Loretta. Would Loretta even talk to her after all these months? she wondered. And Bagley. Would he forgive her for shutting him out of her life? Maybe this trip was a big mistake. Maybe they had forgotten her just like she tried to forget them. She moved over to make room for a heavy lady dressed in navy pants and shirt.

"Thank you." She smiled at Julie and then bent down to take off her shoes. "Whew," she said, leaning back. "Poor dogs. They was killing me."

Julie smiled back and looked out the window.

"Like getting out of jail," she said.

Julie looked back. The lady was wiggling her toes back and forth under gray wool socks. "My dad hates to wear shoes, too," she said. "He wears bedroom slippers all the time—even to work."

"Lucky stiff." She bent over again and rubbed her toes. "I work outside so I gotta wear shoes."

"Umm." Julie wondered what the lady did.

"Car wash," she said. "Ever go to Rainbow, up on Sumpter? I'm the one at the end with the towels."

Julie nodded. "My dad goes there just about every week. In a green Lincoln?"

The lady sat up and smiled. "Oh yeah. The guy wearing the bedroom slippers."

They both started laughing and for a few minutes, Julie forgot about Loretta and Bagley. Then the lady sat back and closed her eyes. Julie looked out the window again, counting the streets the way she used to, remembering how her heart lifted as the bus approached Penny Lane. "Next stop," she whispered to herself and she suddenly felt eager. They passed Sugnet School where Bagley went; Julie pressed her face to the window looking for him. But it was Saturday, she thought, sitting back. He would be in his room, gluing a kite together.

She imagined him practically leaping out of his wheelchair when he saw her. Loretta would be on the Dreamlines talking to someone, fingering her necklaces, and then, like in a movie, she would look up and Julie would be there. Loretta would drop the phone and stand up and they would hug and jump up and down and promise never to be separated again. And Julie would invite Loretta and Bagley over for dinner with her mom and dad and everyone would forgive everyone. They would be like a big family. "Please, God," she whispered when the bus stopped at Penny Lane.

"Watch my dogs," the fat lady said when Julie stood up. She was laughing and Julie laughed, too, giving her a little wave as she got off the bus.

She was surprised that there was no one in the parking lot at Ike's. The metal potatoburger sign clattered back and forth in the wind and leaves from across the street blew up against the front door. She looked for Ike in the window, but instead saw a sign in black marker. CLOSED FOR GOOD.

"Oh, no," she said, staring at the small green building. What had happened to Ike's dream of turning the world into potatoburger lovers? She was going to take Loretta and Bagley there to eat someday. Now they never would. Poor Ike, she thought, looking up and down the street for his yellow-and-black car.

A lady and a little boy raking leaves waved at her; Julie waved back. Ahead, the leaves were six inches deep in Loretta's yard. They could do that, she thought—bundle Bagley up and bring him outside while she and Loretta raked. Or if Loretta was on the phones, Julie would do it. There would be time to see Loretta and time to rake leaves.

She hurried down the street and turned up the walk in front of the big old house, kicking through the leaves. Was Loretta watching her through the window, thinking, Here comes my daughter, here comes Jewel at last? Giddy with nervous energy, Julie bent down and scooped up an armful of leaves, then flung them skyward. "Here I am!" she yelled, running through the shower of red and yellow leaves up to the door. "Here I am!" she yelled again, rushing in, trailing a bright ribbon of leaves.

There was nothing in the room. The tables were gone; so were the phones. No beanbags, no throne chair, no furnishings of any kind. Even the dingy rag rug where she had laid Bagley down that day in July had been taken away. Only the THE QUEEN OF DREAMLAND sign on the wall told her where she was.

Julie felt like a giant hand had reached into her chest and squeezed her heart down to the size of a marble. "Loretta!" she yelled. "Bagley!"

Racing down the hall into the kitchen she found the cupboard doors all flung open, revealing shelf after shelf of emptiness. Not a plate, not a cup, not a canister of flour. The counters were bare except for a splotch of red or purple stain here and there—reminders of Mrs. Og's berry pies. On the floor a roll of paper towels had been left rolled out like a green-and-white-checked runner. From the sink came the steady plop, plop, plop of the leaky faucet, the only sound in the room. "Mrs. Og?" Julie whispered, suddenly afraid of her own voice. She moved to the pantry doorway—Bagley's bedroom—hesitated, then opened the door. The washers and dryers were still there, but the wire baskets were tipped over. Bagley's bed was gone; so were his desk and the flotilla of kites he hung from the ceiling. Scraps of red paper were scattered across the floor. Some jelly beans sat in a clump in the corner. Was this all that was left of the boy who lived in this room? Julie couldn't even say his name. She put her hand over her mouth.

Down the back hall she ran, to the basement steps. She flicked the light switch on and off. Nothing happened. "Cramp!" she called down into the darkness. But the echo of her own voice came faintly back, bouncing off the emptiness of the walls, the floor, the ceiling.

Still not believing, Julie ran back down the hall and through the living room, to the other hall and the circus room, the room where she first knew Loretta so long ago. It was unchanged. The room, still hung with orange fabric felt safe, familiar to her. She touched the material, closed her eyes, and brushed her cheek against the drapery, trying to picture Loretta sitting there in her folding chair, chewing gum, waiting for her.

Finally, she allowed herself to think it. Loretta was gone. Bagley was gone. She sank down onto the dusty wood floor and put her hands over her eyes. But she couldn't stop the hot tears rising from a great well of bitterness in her heart. *Gone.* Without a word, without even a trace. Not a scrap of paper to say where they were, to say, "I miss you, Jewel." That they could do that to her, just walk away, was more than she could bear. As if she were nothing more than a passing acquaintance, someone they had run into at the post office. She had allowed herself to believe that Loretta was her mother, the one who loved her best, who had come back for her after all these years because of that lonely ache, the one Julie knew so well.

She hit the wood floor with her fists, her knuckles taking the sharp pain of the blow. "Stupid," she said. "Stupid jerk-face moron." Loretta was only a dream that Julie had created. Bagley, too. They were just people—a mother and son—who moved here and then moved away. What did that have to do with her? They were like that lady and her son raking leaves. They forgot Julie the instant she walked by. That's how it was. Loretta and Bagley were in another town, miles away. Loretta was thinking up a new scam to cheat people out of their money.

"Cheat!" she said, snuffing loudly. "Cheat, cheat, liar, liar." She pulled a hunk of the orange fabric away from the wall and blew her nose on it. There was a noise behind her. Julie turned and her heart stopped. Loretta stood in the doorway, teetering on shiny gold heels.

Julie wiped her face with both hands and put her glasses back on. "Wh-where did you come from?"

"Highway sixteen, right at Ortonville Road. That's where I got your message."

"What're you talking about," Julie muttered, looking away.

Loretta put her hands on her hips and narrowed her eyes. "Well, I guess you sent me a message or I wouldn't of come back all that way."

"Are you moving or something?" Julie asked, trying to sound offhand.

"Moved," Loretta said firmly. "Bagley and Duane are already—"

Julie caught her breath. "Duane?"

"I'm married, Jewel. I'm Mrs. Duane Cabot Forester the first. See." She held out her left hand, which was dwarfed by an enormous diamond. "We had a nice church wedding with gardenias and white bows on all the pews and lit candles. Too bad you weren't there," she added sharply.

Julie shrugged, but she felt like she had been run over by a locomotive. Loretta had turned her back on her, had made a new life for herself, entirely apart from Julie, as though Loretta had no daughter to consider when she went off and attached herself to some perfect stranger. Julie raised her eyes and studied the ceiling, the round, orange knob of fabric at the center, trying to calm herself, making herself think of oranges, of anything but Mrs. Duane Cabot Forester.

"I don't care if you don't like him, Jewel, one bit. He's very proper and he's kind to Bagley and he's—"

"Yeah, you told me—rich."

Loretta's gray eyes glittered. "Bagley's operation is scheduled for before Christmas. Duane's business covers everything, including meals."

Julie nodded, tight-lipped. "I'm glad for Bagley and I'm—I'm glad for you. I hope you'll all live happily ever after," she added, lifting her chin.

"So—" Loretta said, flinging back her hair. She took a silk hanky out of the breast pocket of her orange dress, then a foil-wrapped stick of gum. She stuffed the hanky back in her pocket and unwrapped the gum, rolled it up, and plopped it in her mouth. "You didn't send me the message about coming back?"

Julie shook her head.

"Well," she said, "and here I thought you did." She twitched her orange belt back and forth. "I gotta get along."

Julie sat there in the middle of the floor and watched her go, heard her heels clicking down the hall when she couldn't see her anymore. She wiped her cheeks again with the palms of her hands. It was over, she thought. Loretta was really out of her life. She looked up at the orange ceiling, picturing Loretta driving down the road in her orange dress, the window open so that her hair was blowing to one side. Chewing gum. And she heard her voice saying, "Your heart calls to me; I don't care if it's at the bottom of a well—I hear it, Jewel. We're connected forever."

Her mistake washed over her like scalding water. She *had* sent for Loretta. Like a spider throwing a little silken thread, she had wanted to catch Loretta, catch Bagley, too. They belonged to her as much as to anyone. And now, she had let the thread break, let them go. Did she have so many precious things in her life that she could afford to lose these two?

"Loretta!" She got to her feet, her heart overflowing with what she had forgotten to say. If she yelled loud enough, ran fast enough, maybe she could catch her. "Loretta!" She would take a cab to Highway 61 and Ortonville Road and stand in the road, waving her red beret until Loretta came. She raced down the hall and around the corner into the living room.

There, in the window, framed by the October light, stood Loretta. Waiting for her.

Julie kept going right into Loretta's arms.

"I knew you sent that message, Jewel." She stroked Julie's hair.

"I did," Julie choked out. "I love you, Loretta. I didn't mean to hurt you."

"Pssh," Loretta said. "Let's not talk hurts anymore, Jewel. I love you and you love me. We got our lives to lead. They're waiting for us down in Ohio. Oh, Cramp and Mrs. Og have gone off but Bagley and Duane—wait till they see you."

Julie drew back. "Wh-what?"

"That's what I came back for, Jewel." She took Julie's face in her hands, her own face flushed with excitement. "You!" She giggled. "See—we got this awful huge house, real modern, with a pink bedroom upstairs that looks onto a swimming pool bigger than yours. And that room's for you, Jewel. You'll have your own phone and—"

Julie stared at Loretta's glowing face. "You mean—leave my mom and dad and go live with you?"

Loretta nodded, her curls flying. "Oh, sure, you'll want to come back here for visits, summer vacations and stuff. Of course, Wayne and Mame'll want to see you. But you'll be my daughter again just like you were meant to be."

"Oh, Loretta, I—" Julie shook her head, afraid her words would crush this moment of happiness. "I love you, Loretta. I've loved you from the second I took a breath and saw you looking down at me. I think for fourteen years I carried that thought in my heart, wanting more than anything for you to love me back—to really, really want me."

"Why, I never once stopped loving you, Jewel. Not for a microsecond. That's why I—and Bagley and Duane—want you to live with us, forever and ever. Everything is slam bang perfect."

"But Loretta—my mom and dad are my—they're just—" A hundred memories raced through Julie's head. The clicking of her father's spoon in his oatmeal bowl every morning, the way he spread jam on her toast so thick it ran down her fingers. Her mother's head, bent in the lamplight, embroidering Julie's name on her sweatshirt. An image came to her of her mother bursting through Loretta's front door, breathless with worry. A thousand times she had rescued Julie from bloody knees, measles, broken hearts. In her worst moments, in her happiest moments, her mother had always been there. And her father. How could it be any other way?

Julie shook her head. "I can't leave them. They're everything I've loved, everything I've ever believed in since I was born. They're—they're my life, Loretta," she said thickly.

Loretta let go of her. She looked at Julie for a long, long moment. There were tears in her eyes as she turned toward the door.

"Wait—will you write me?" Julie asked breathlessly.

" 'Course, silly." She touched Julie's cheek and went out.

Loretta clicked down the sidewalk and opened the door of Duane's black Cadillac.

"Give Bagley a big hug for me," Julie called.

Loretta rolled down the window. "Bye, Jewel."

Julie nodded, unable to say a word as Loretta backed down the drive. But as Loretta pulled out onto the street, Julie began to run.

"Wait!" She ran up to the car window and yanked off the red beret. "Here," she said, unpinning the brooch with trembling fingers. "I want you to have this."

"Aw, Jewel—your pin? I can't take that. It must be worth oodles."

"Yes," Julie said, "yes, you can." Gingerly, she set the jewel into Loretta's upturned hand. "Take it. Keep it forever." She turned away then and didn't turn back until the car was a tiny black dot a long way down the road.

About the Author

INGRID TOMEY grew up in Midland, Michigan, watching her mother pull herself up to the typewriter daily to write everything from children's stories to occult novels. From this example, Ingrid soon began transforming all the events of her life into story and verse. In addition to writing the children's books *Grandfather's Day, Neptune Princess*, and *Savage Carrot*, Ingrid writes for various magazines. She lives in West Bloomfield, Michigan, with her husband Paul.